DATE			

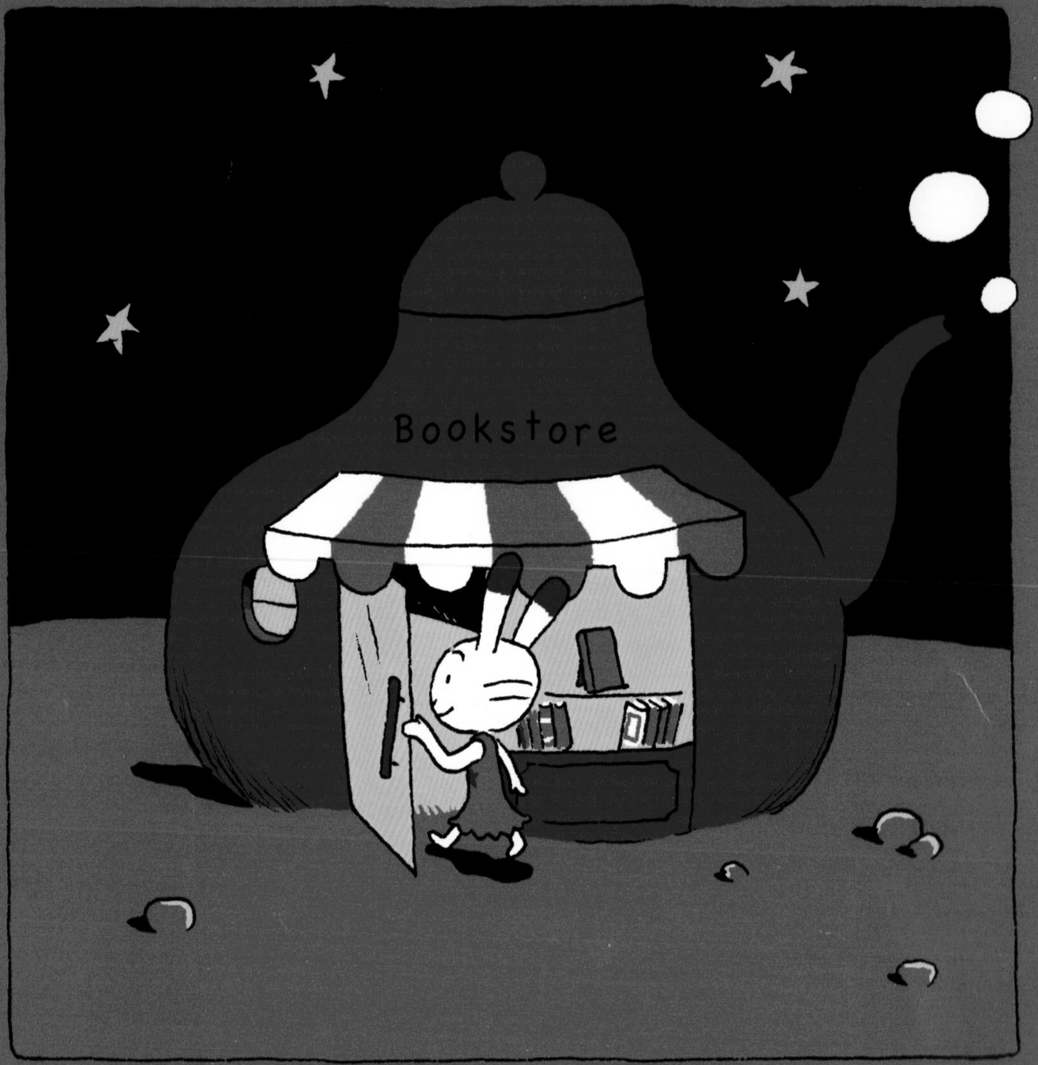
Bookstore

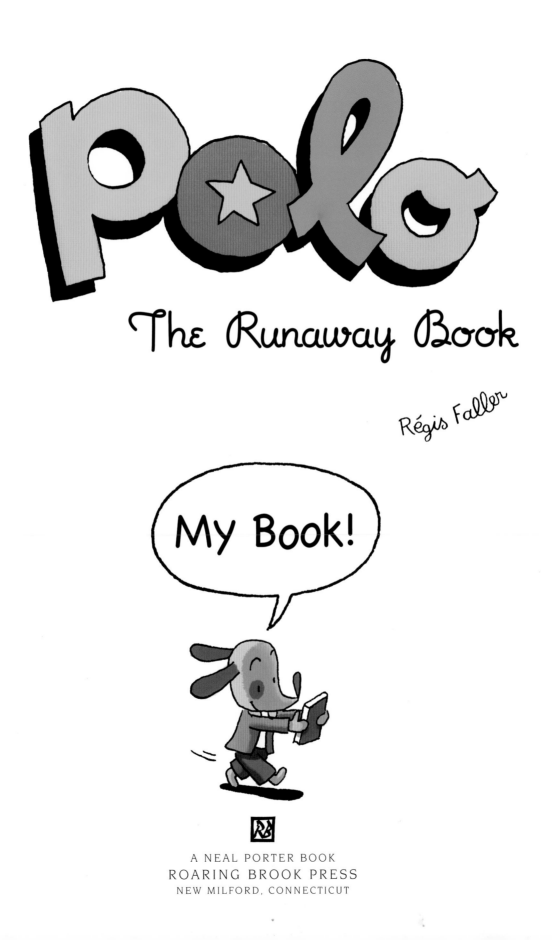

Polo

The Runaway Book

Régis Faller

My Book!

A NEAL PORTER BOOK
ROARING BROOK PRESS
NEW MILFORD, CONNECTICUT

Copyright © 2005 by Régis Faller

A Neal Porter Book

Published by Roaring Brook Press

Roaring Brook Press is a division of Holtzbrinck Publishing Holdings Limited Partnership

143 West Street, New Milford, Connecticut 06776

First published in France by Bayard Éditions Jeunesse

Distributed in Canada by H. B. Fenn and Company Ltd.

Library of Congress Cataloging-in-Publication Data

Faller, Régis.

[Polo, mon livre! English]

Polo: the runaway book / Regis Faller. – 1st American ed.

p. cm.

Summary: While trying to retrieve his new book from a thieving alien,

Polo has a series of adventures and eventually helps the alien and his people.

ISBN-13: 978-1-59643-189-8   ISBN-10: 1-59643-189-X

[1. Dogs—Fiction. 2. Extraterrestrial beings—Fiction. 3. Stories without words.] I. Title.

PZ7.F1886Pol 2007   [E]—dc22   2005055183

Roaring Brook Press books are available for special promotions and premiums.

For details contact: Director of Special Markets, Holtzbrinck Publishers.

First American edition January 2007

Printed in China

2 4 6 8 10 9 7 5 3 1

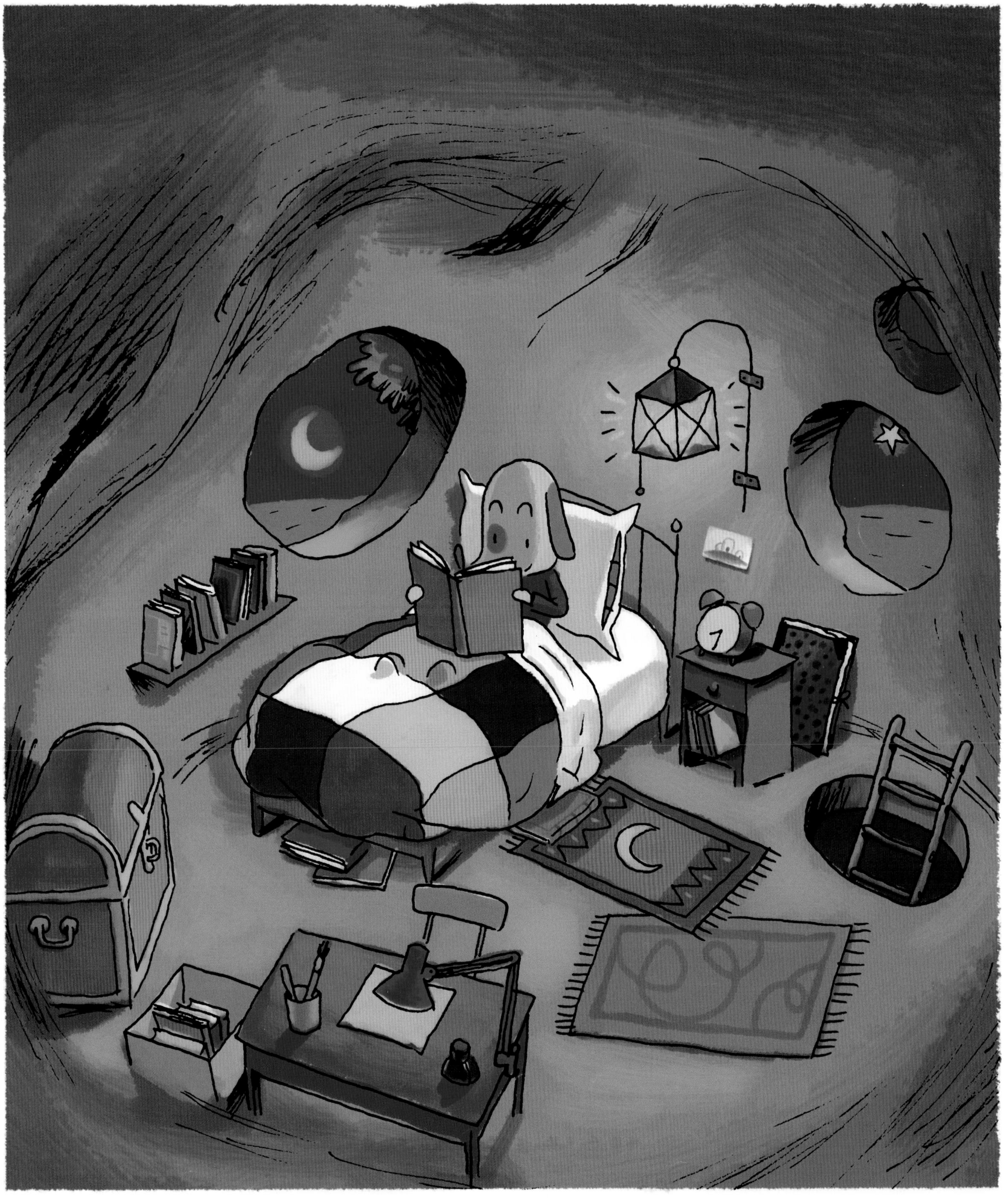

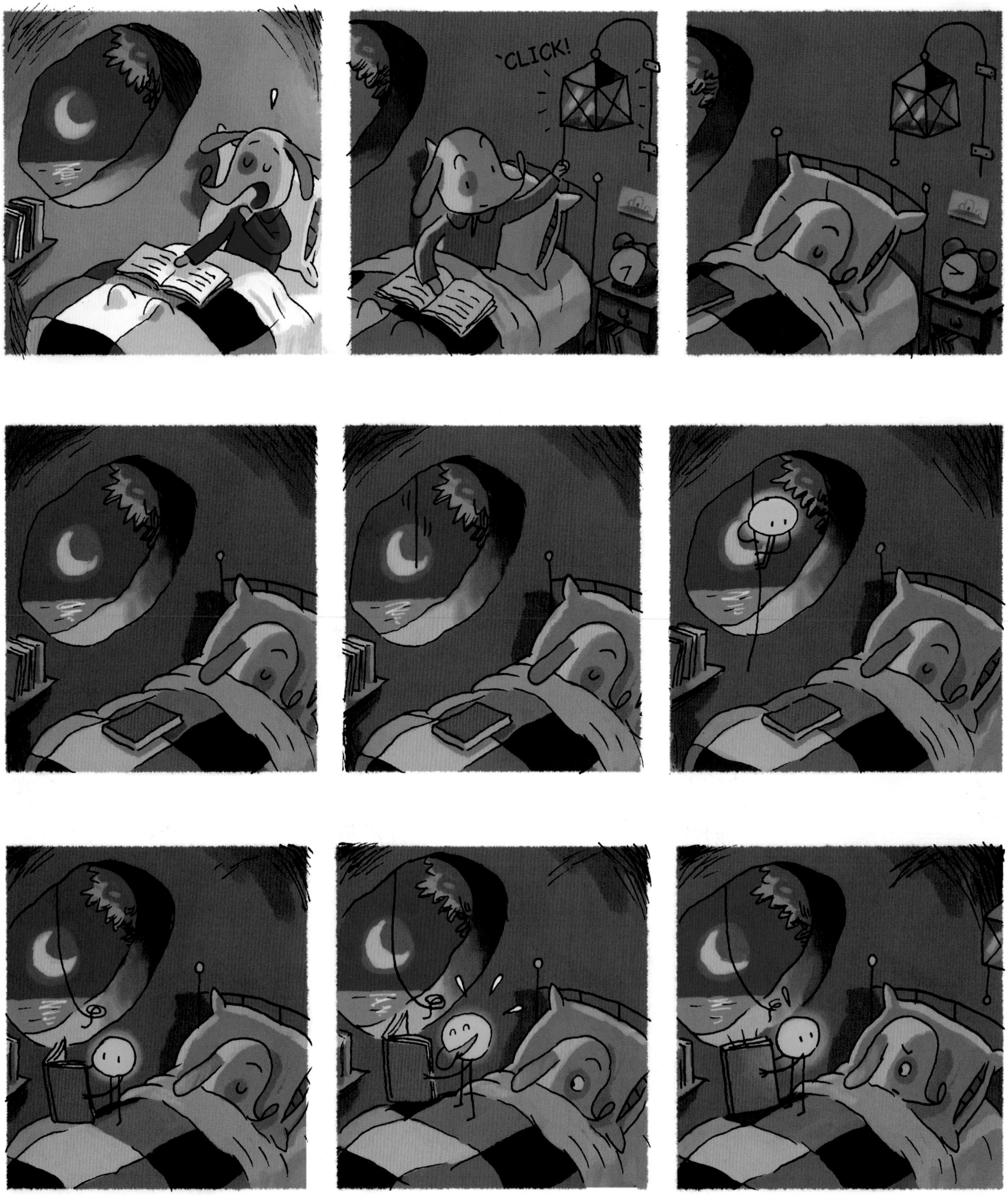
CLICK!

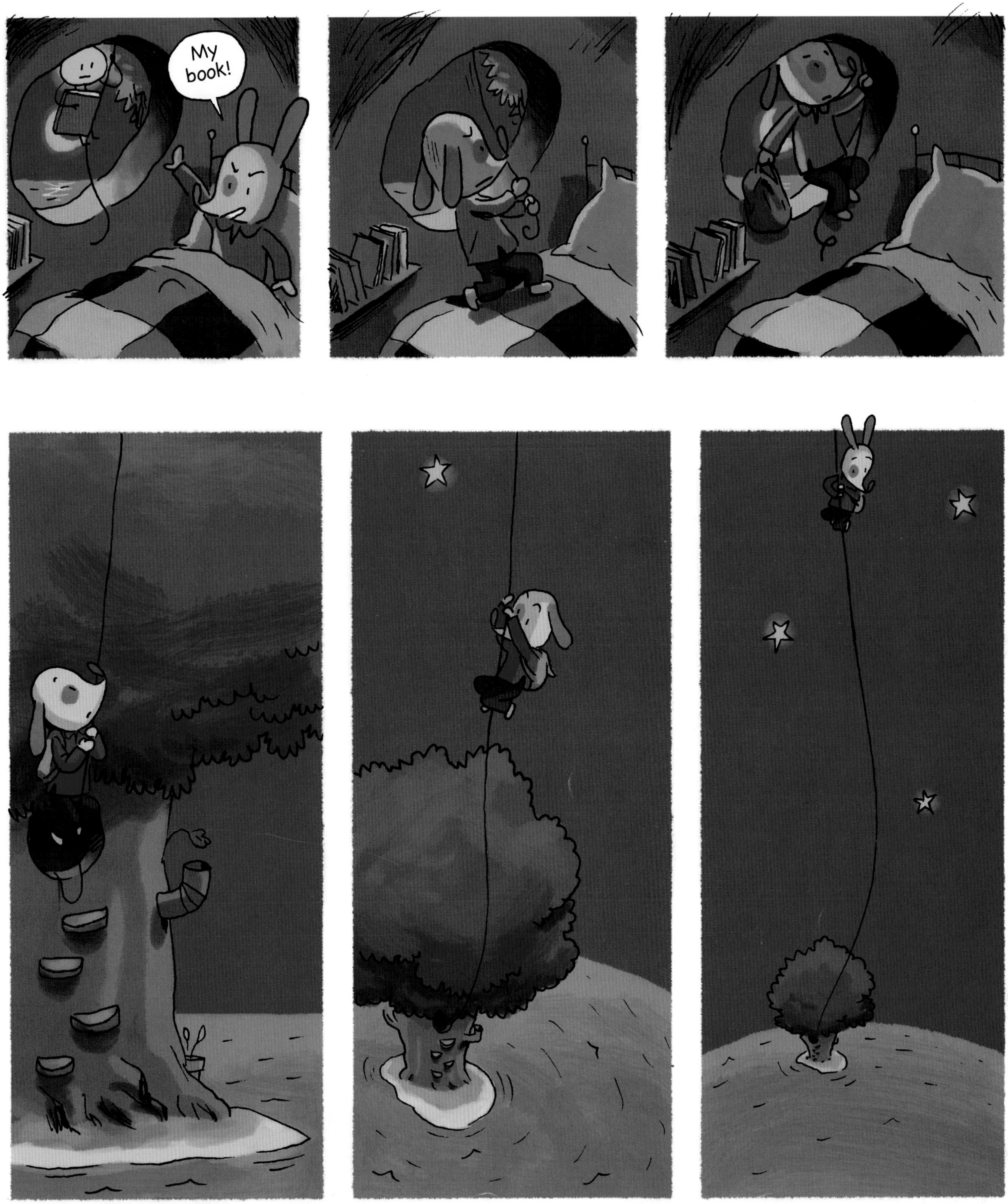
My book!

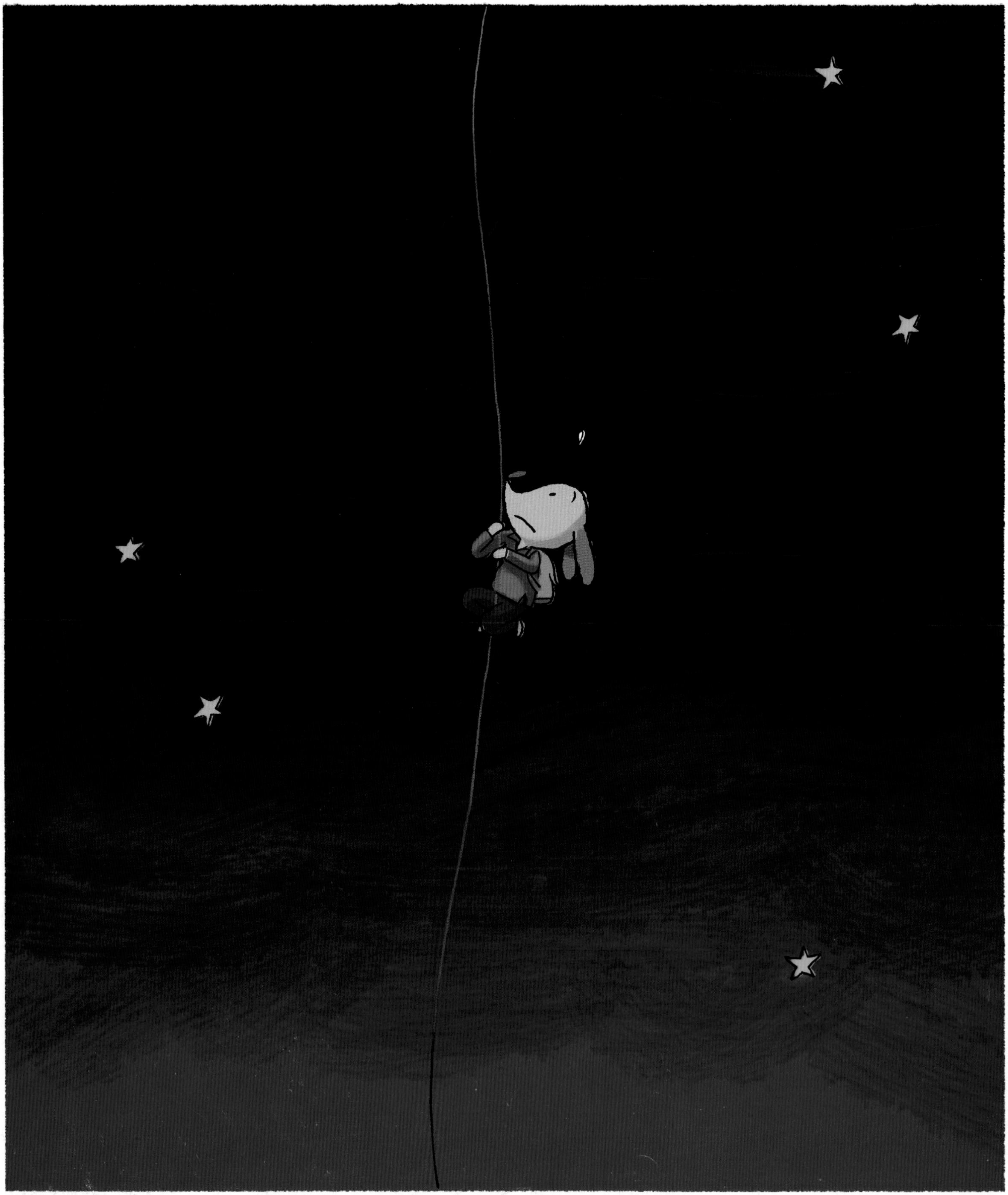

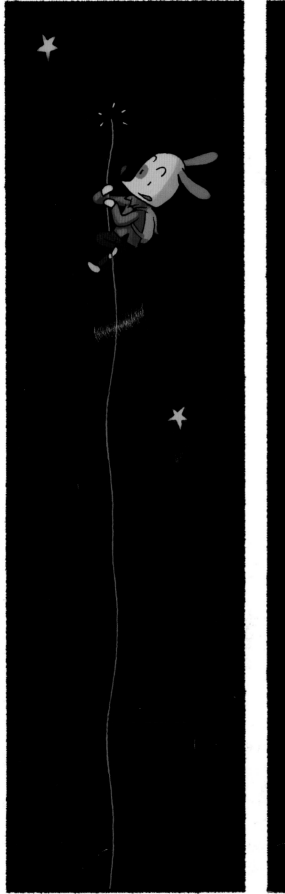

Cotto
Cotton Candy

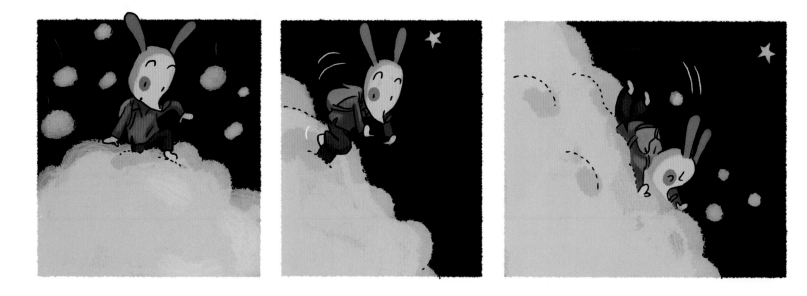

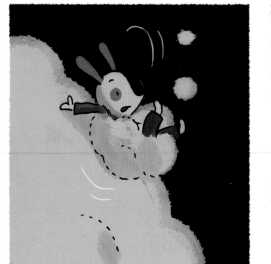

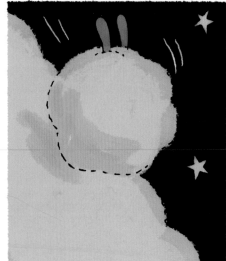

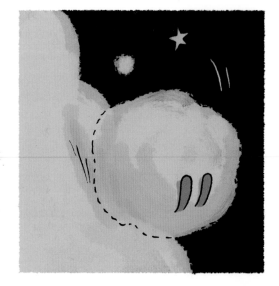

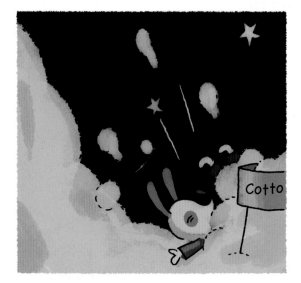

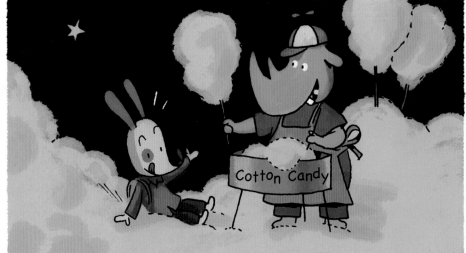

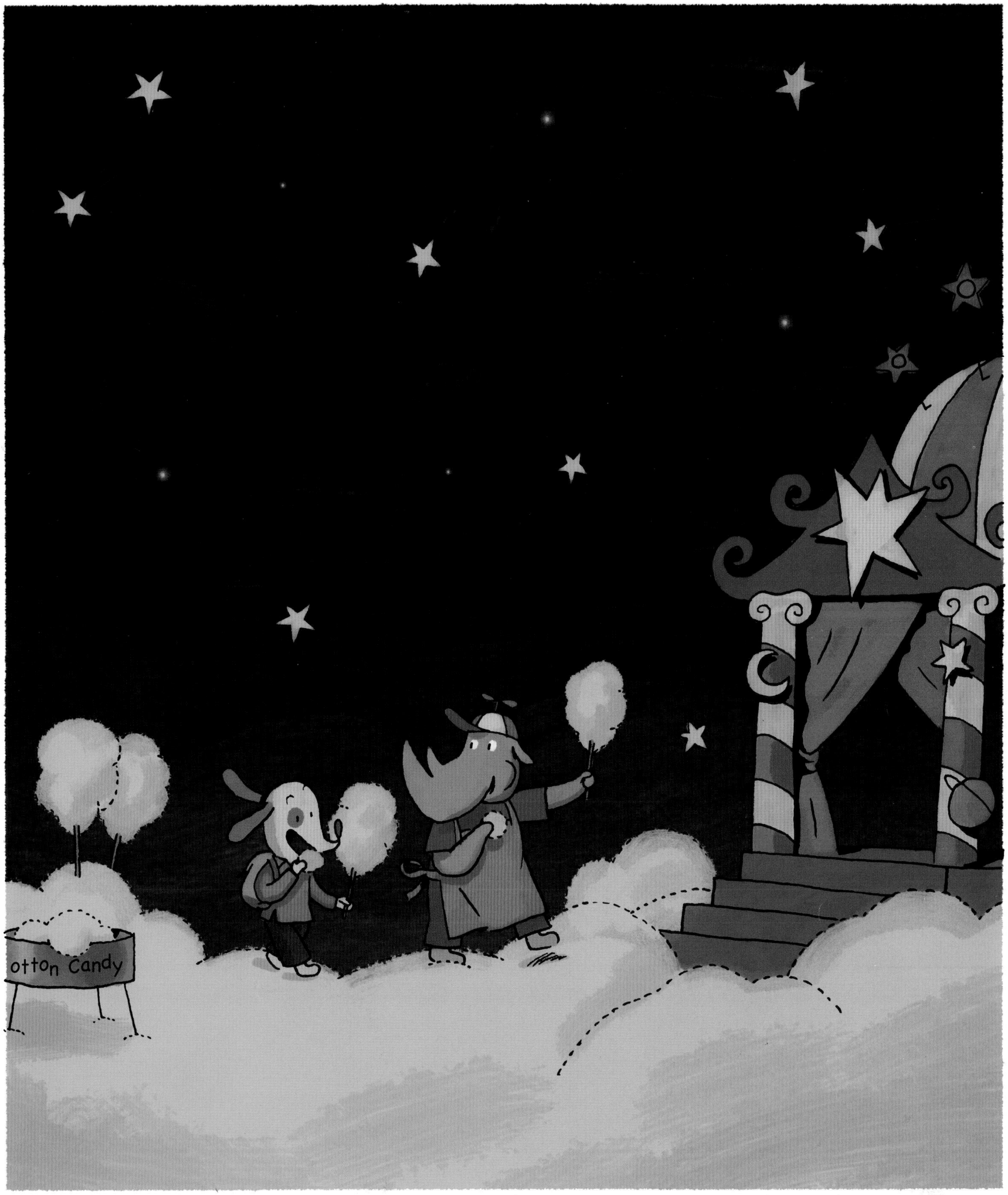
otton Candy

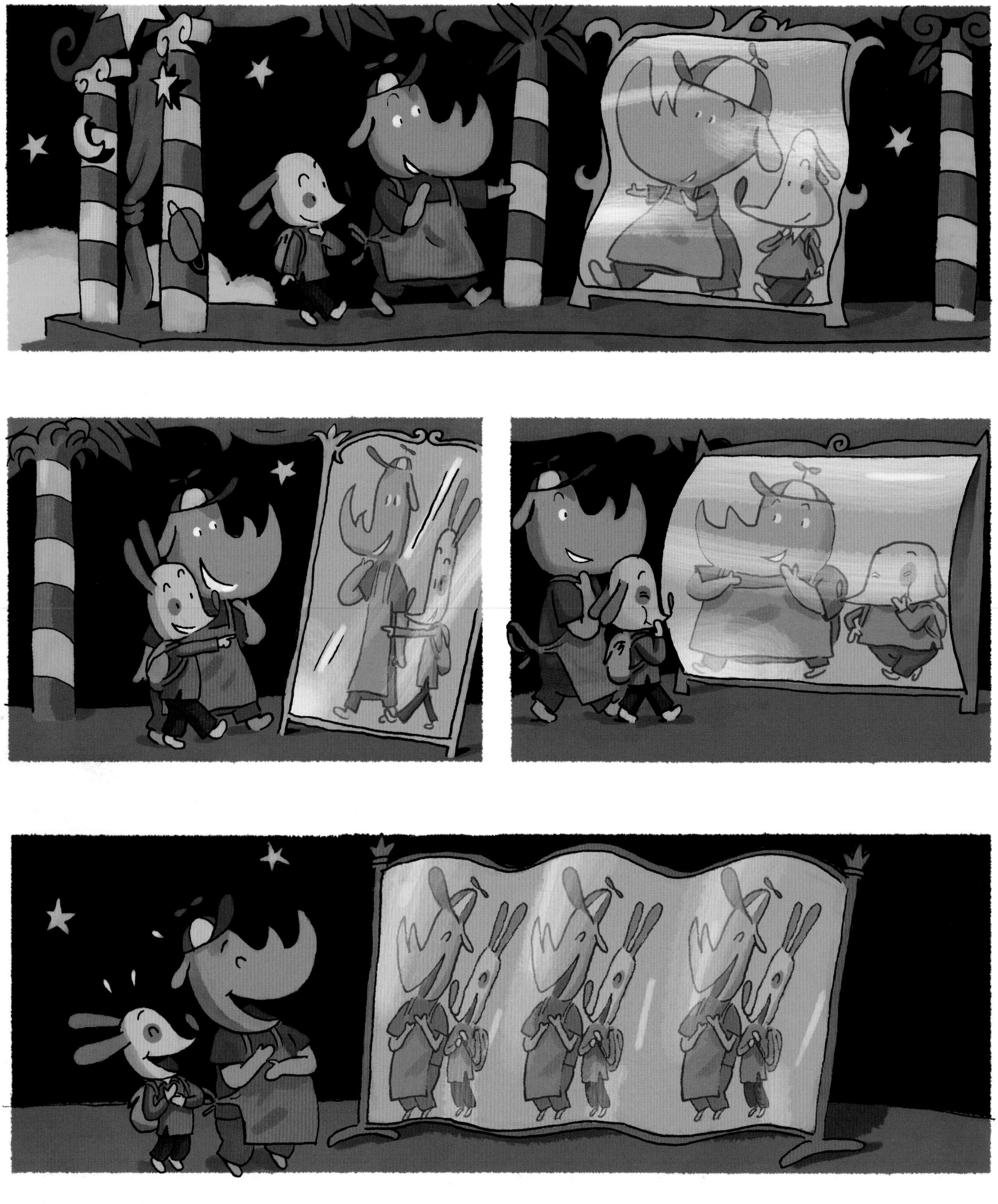

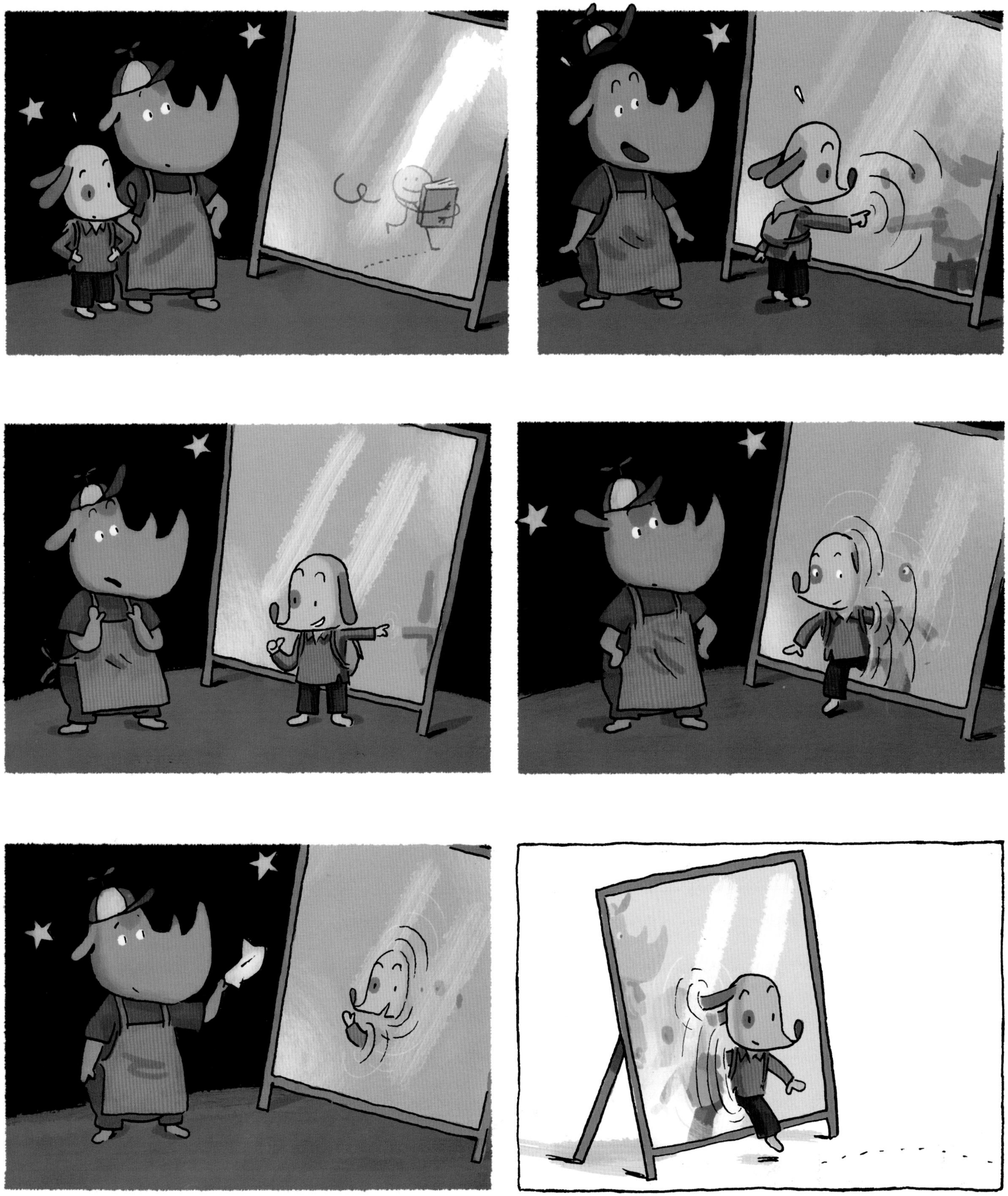

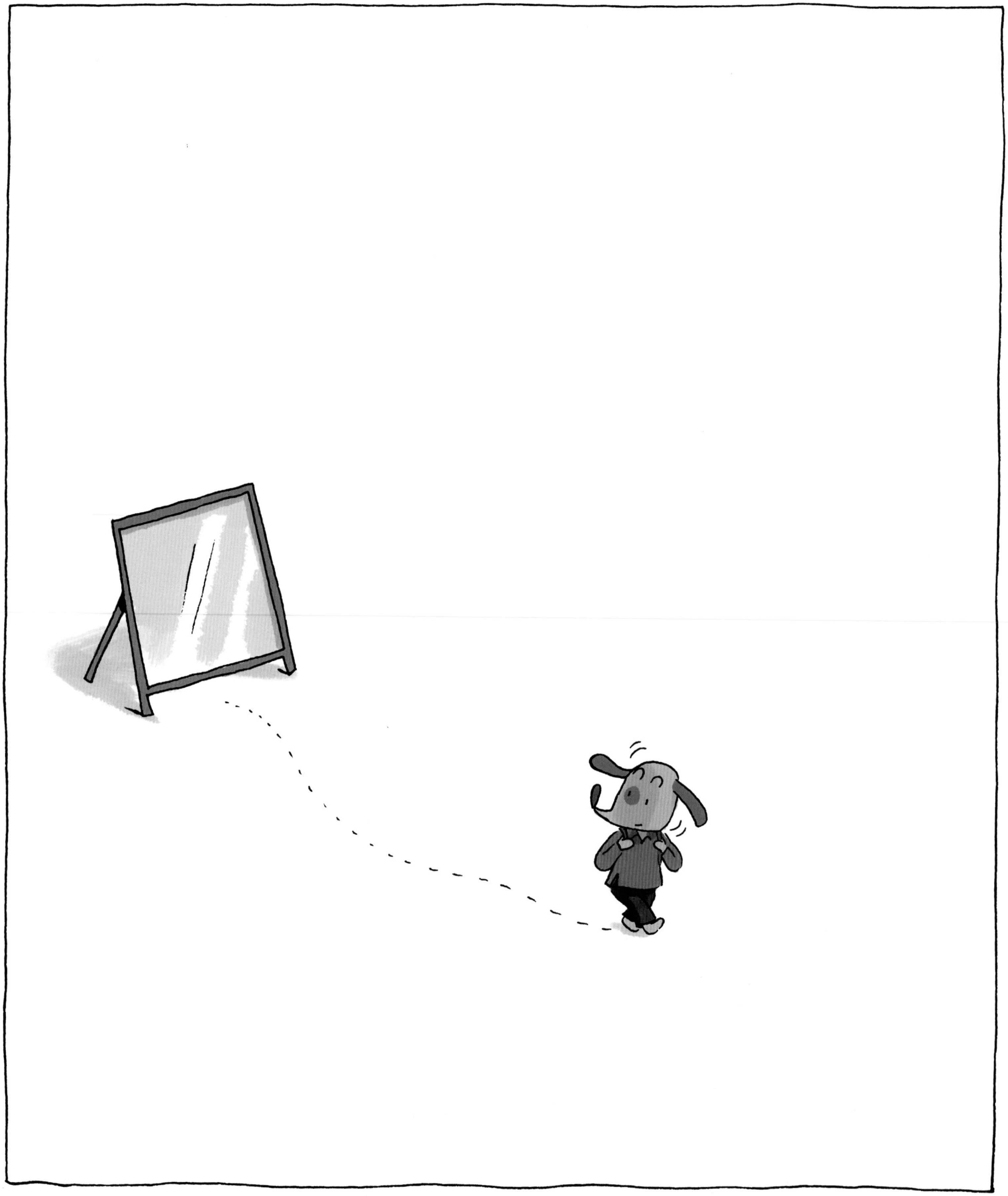

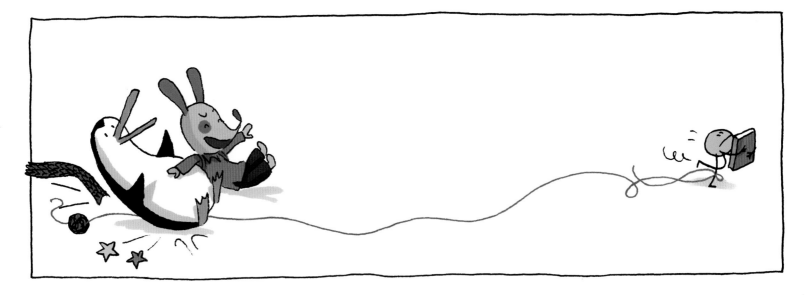

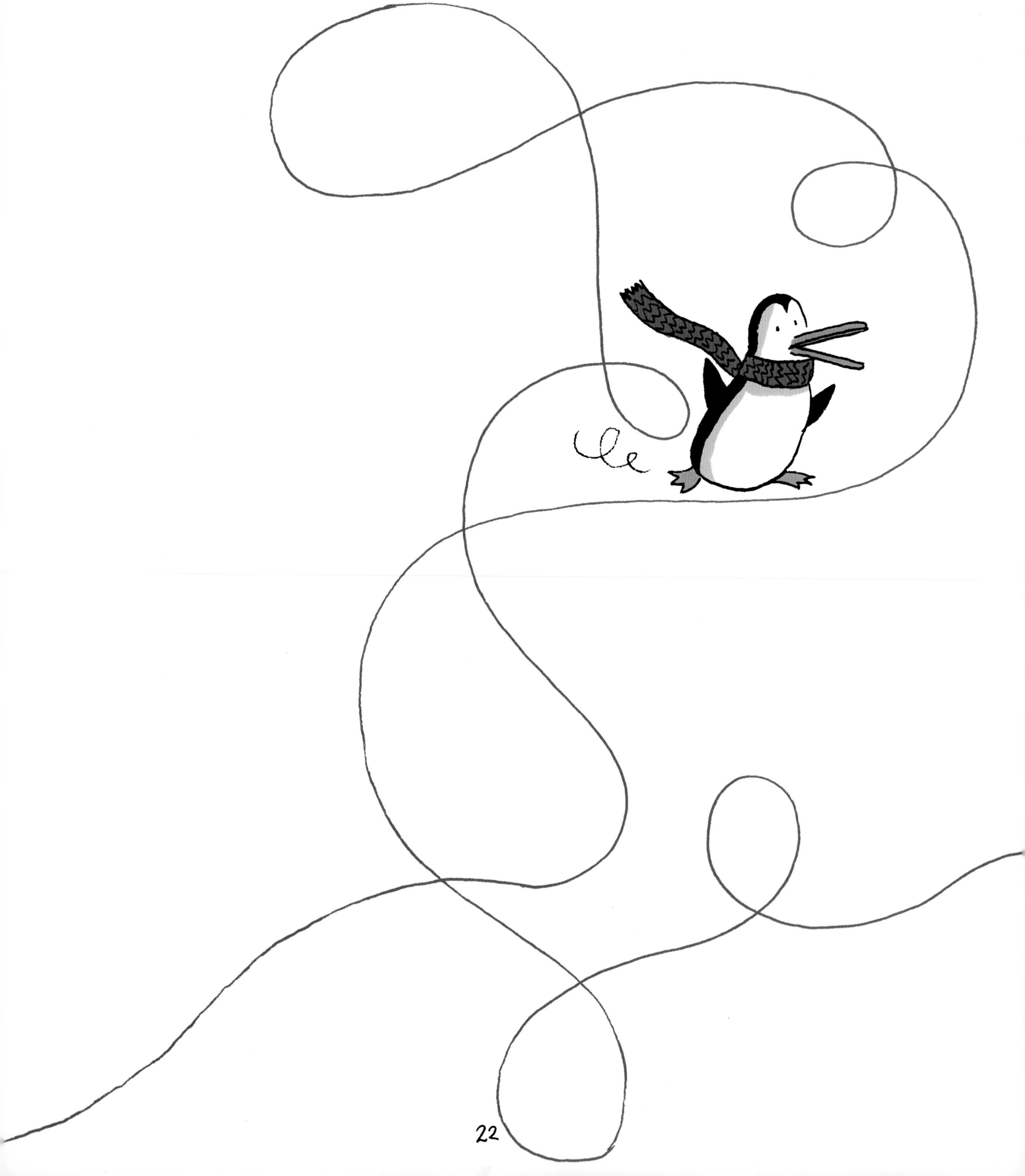

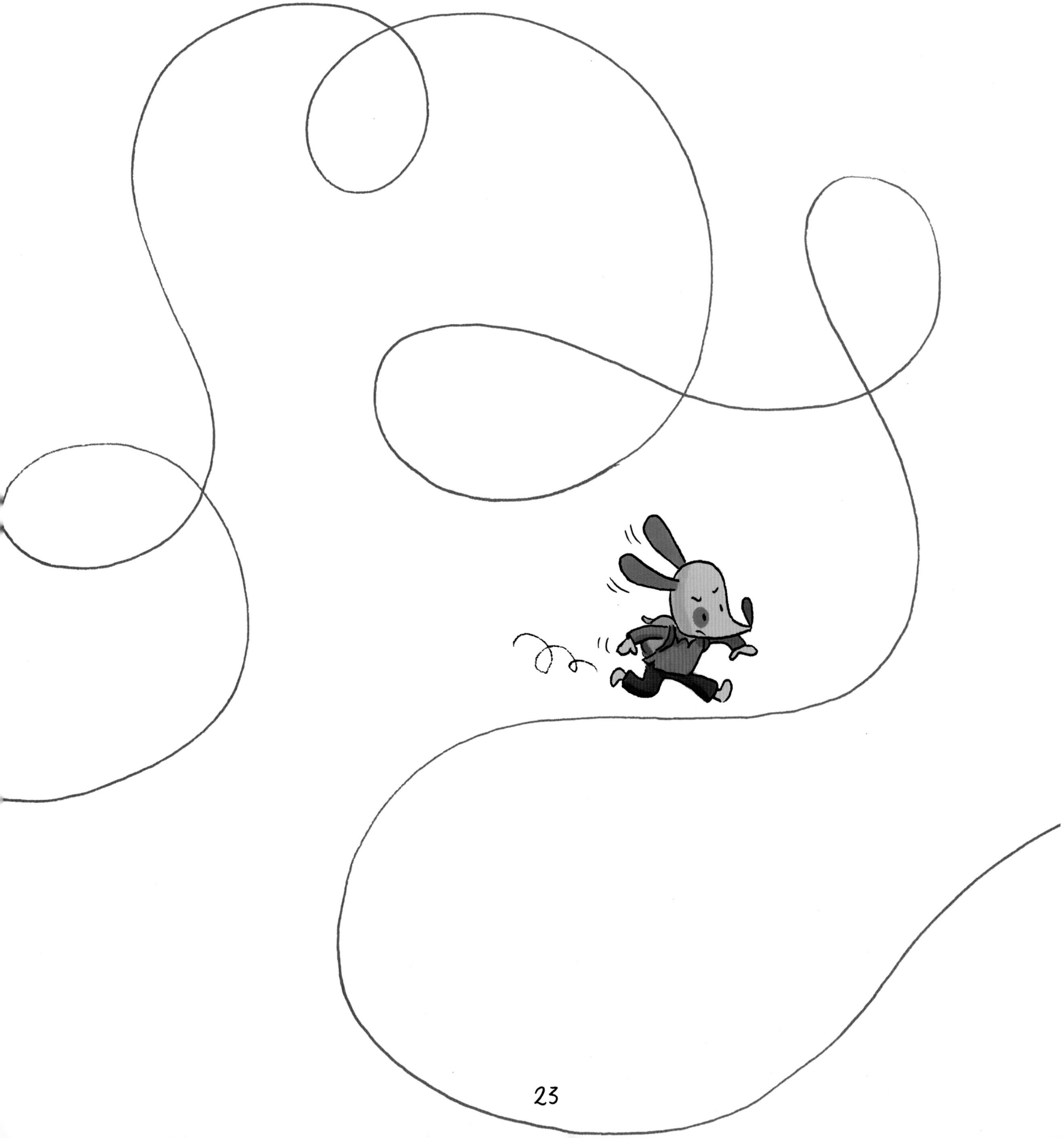

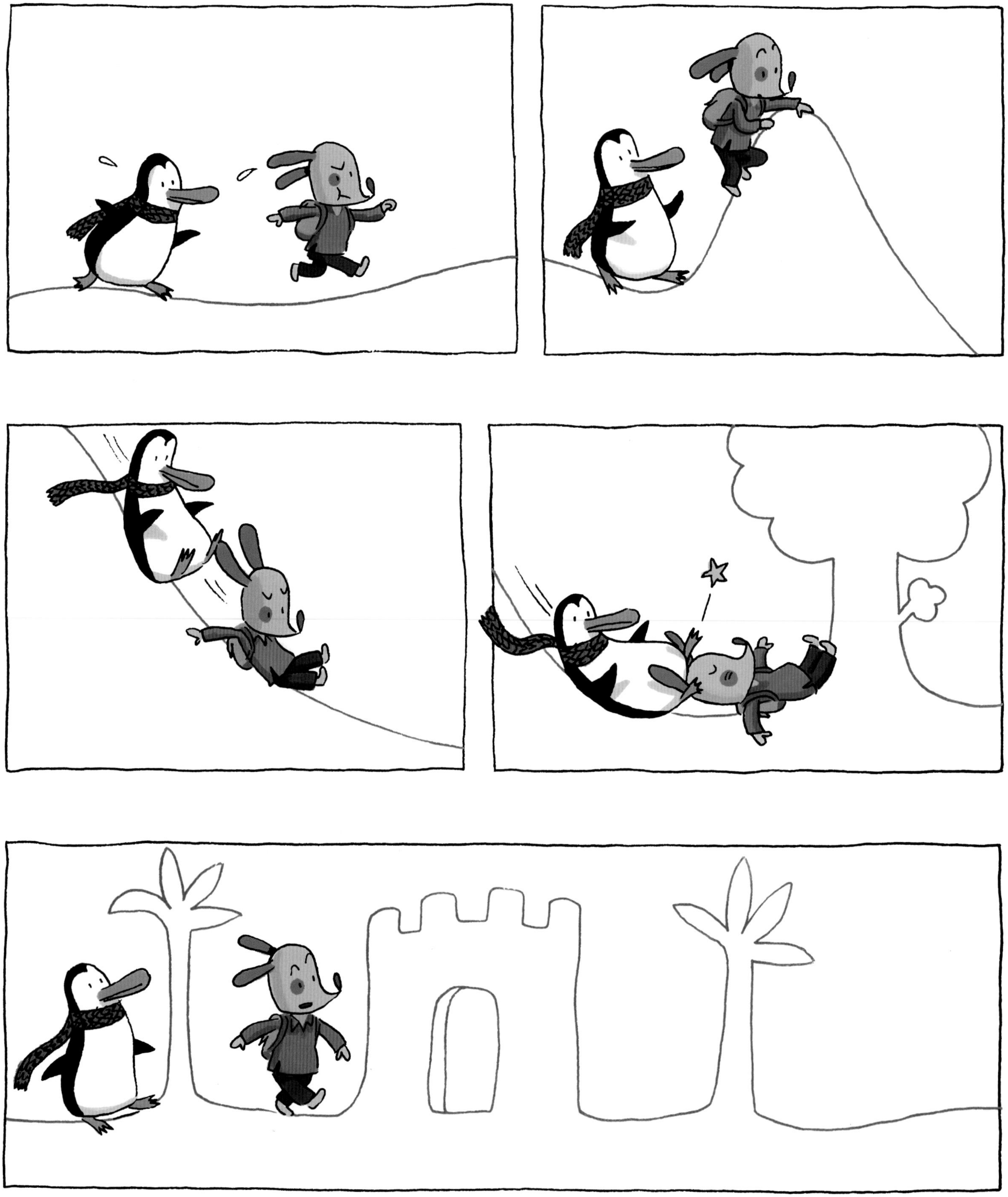

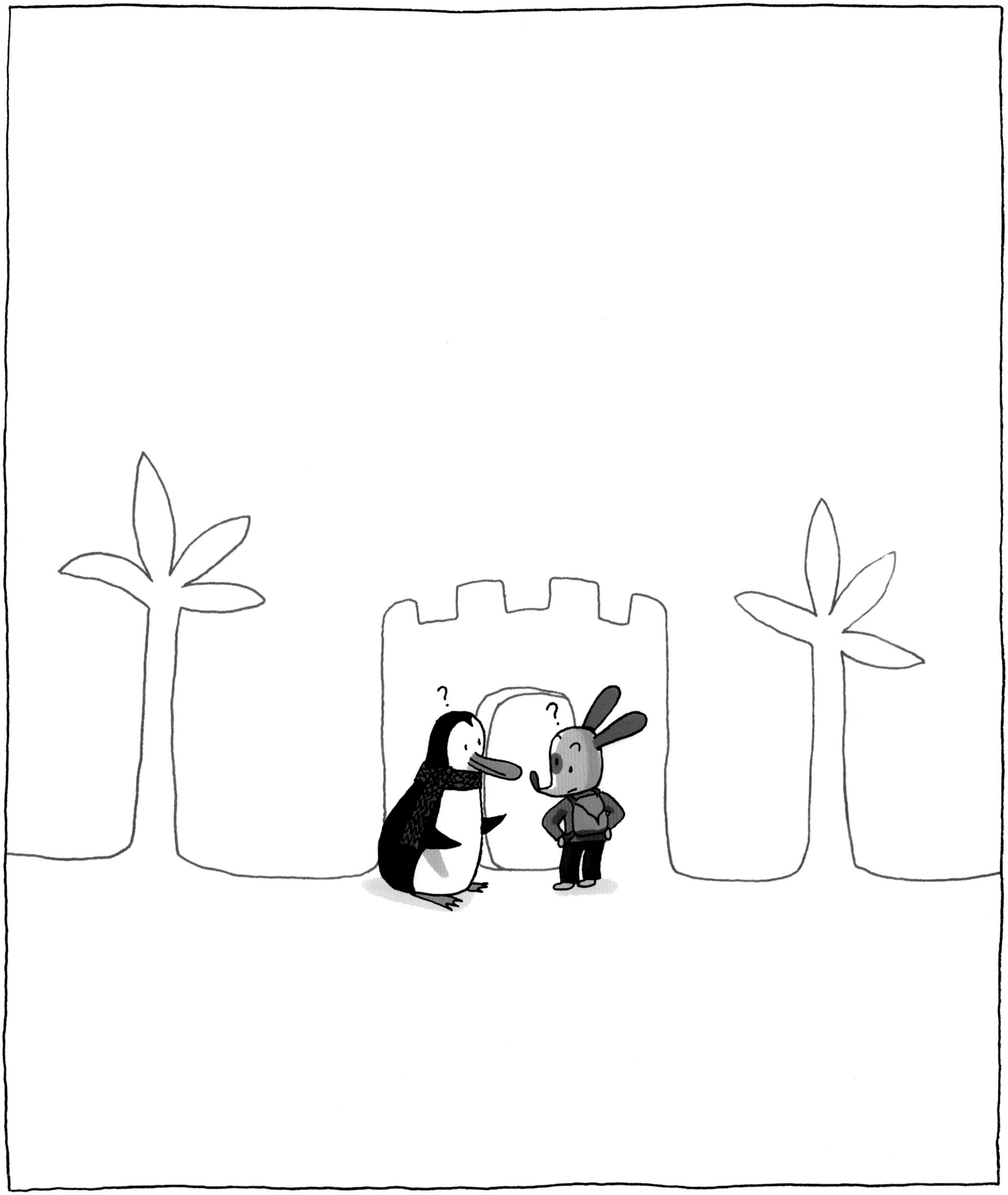
?
?

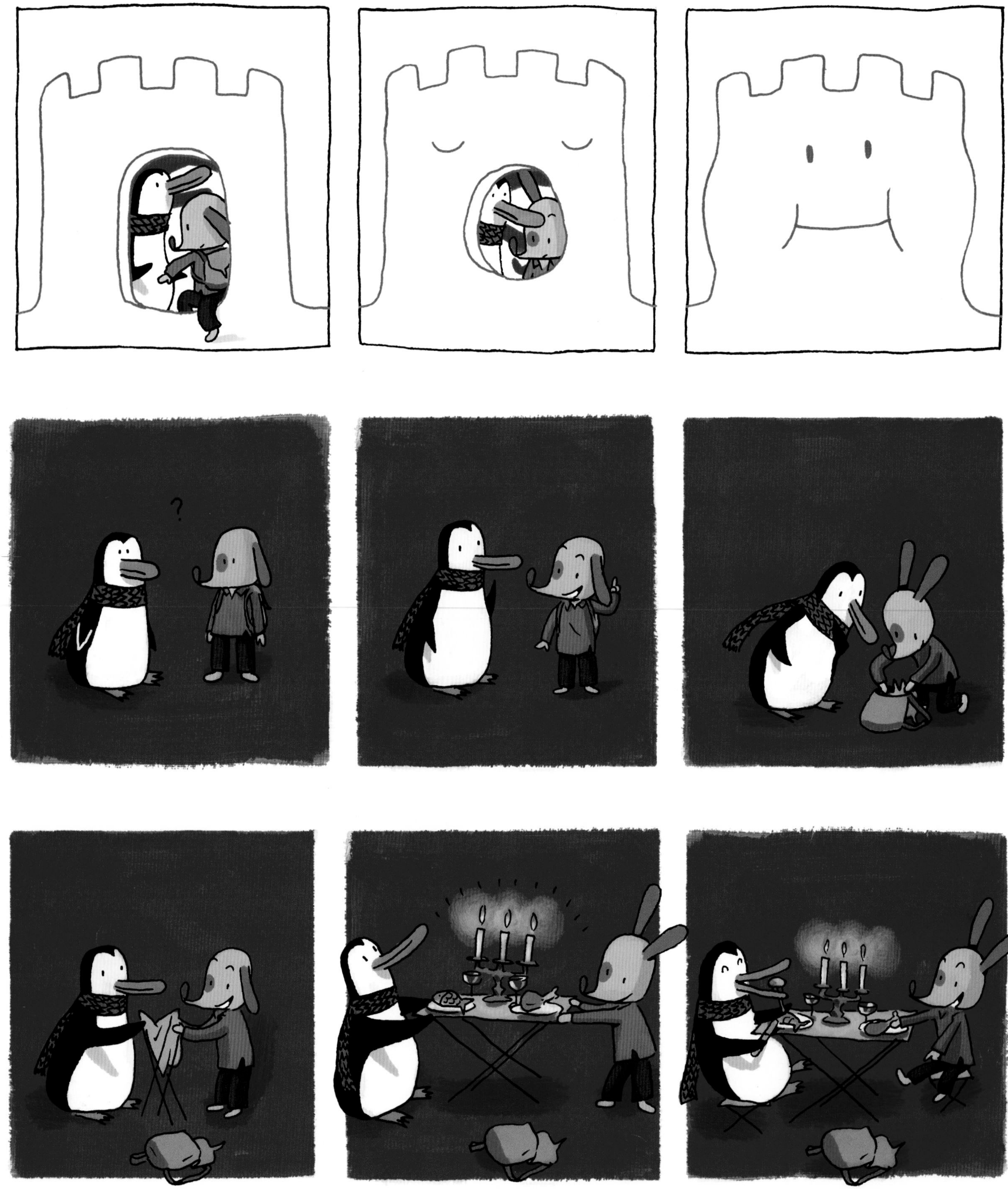
?

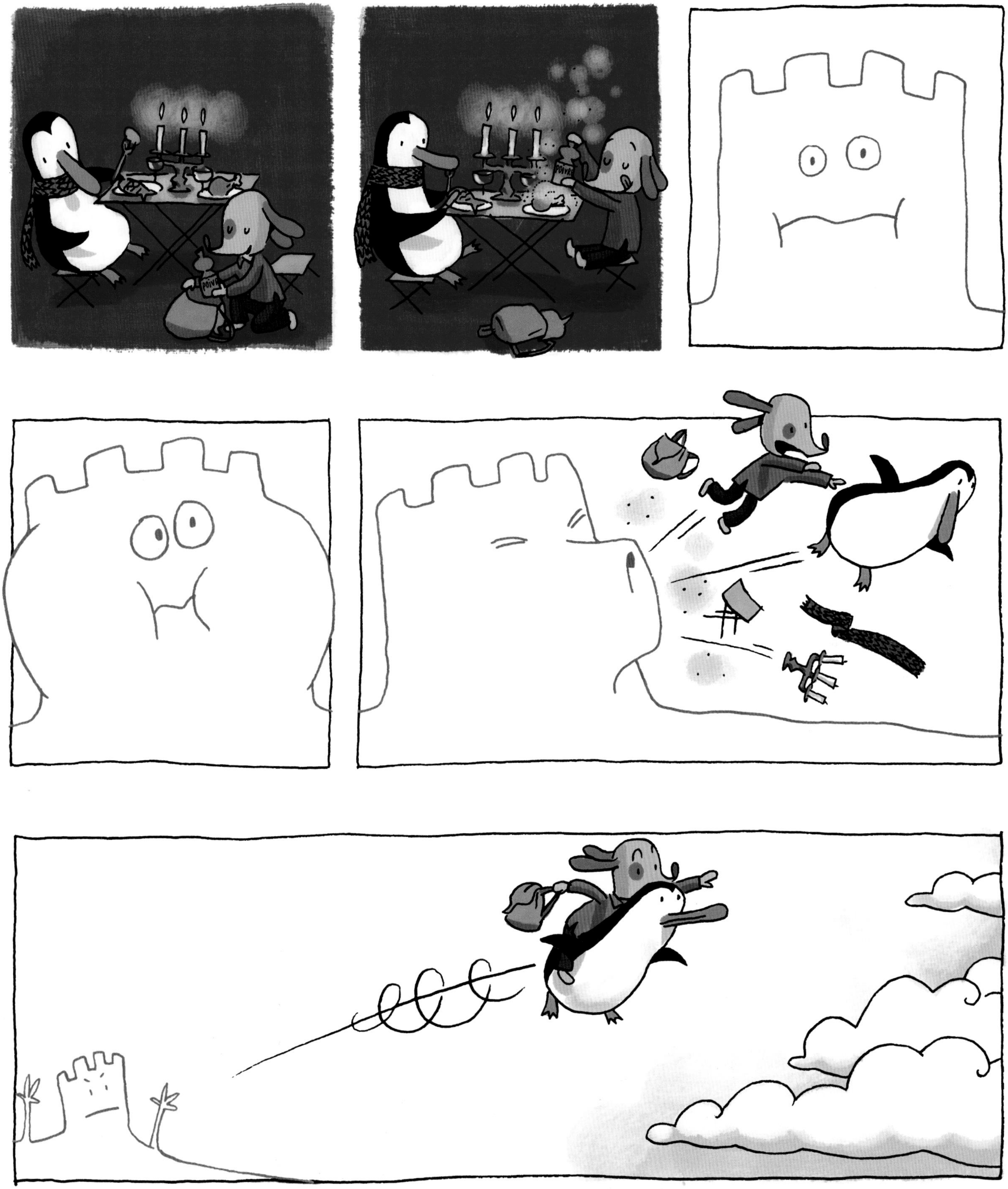

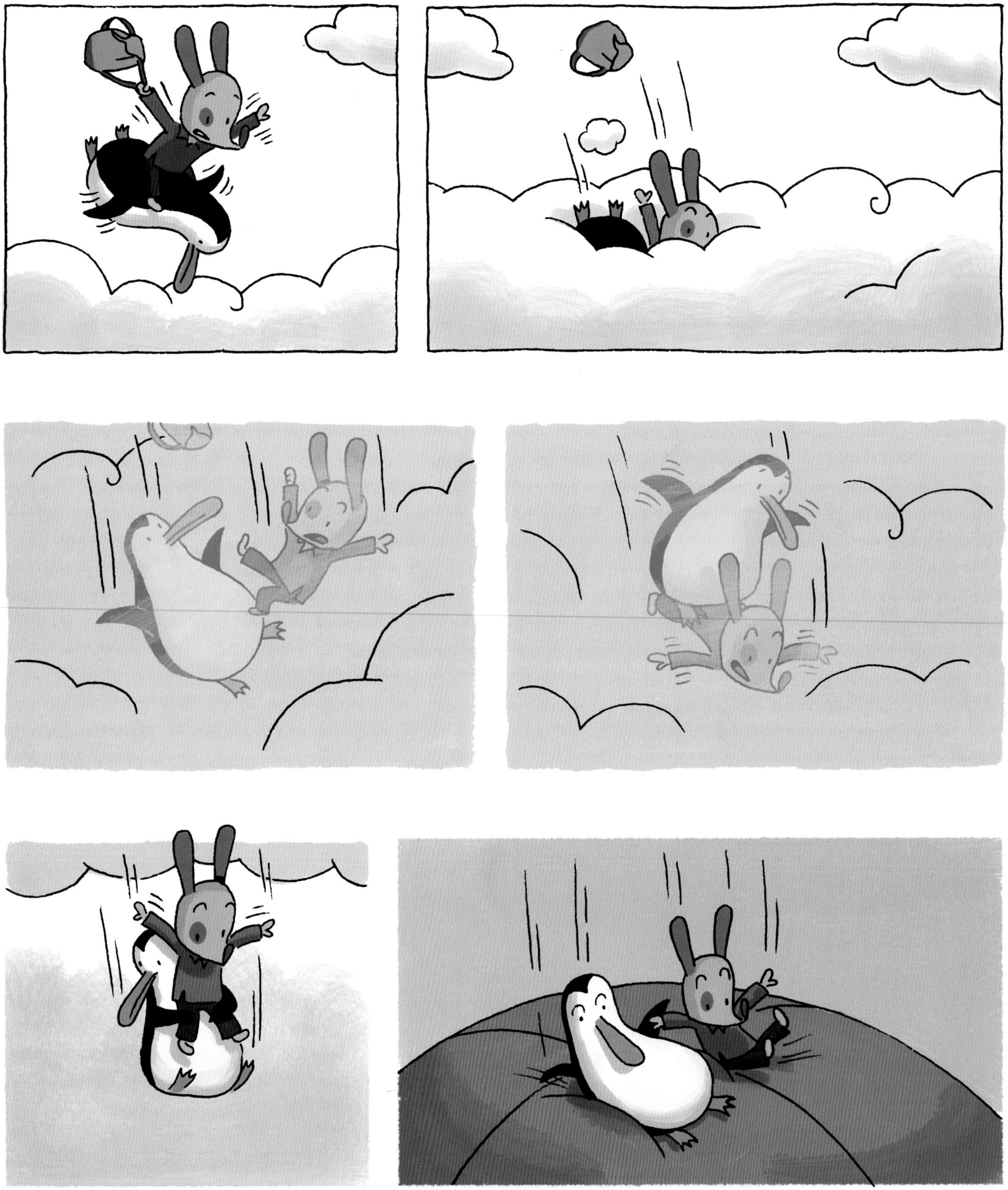

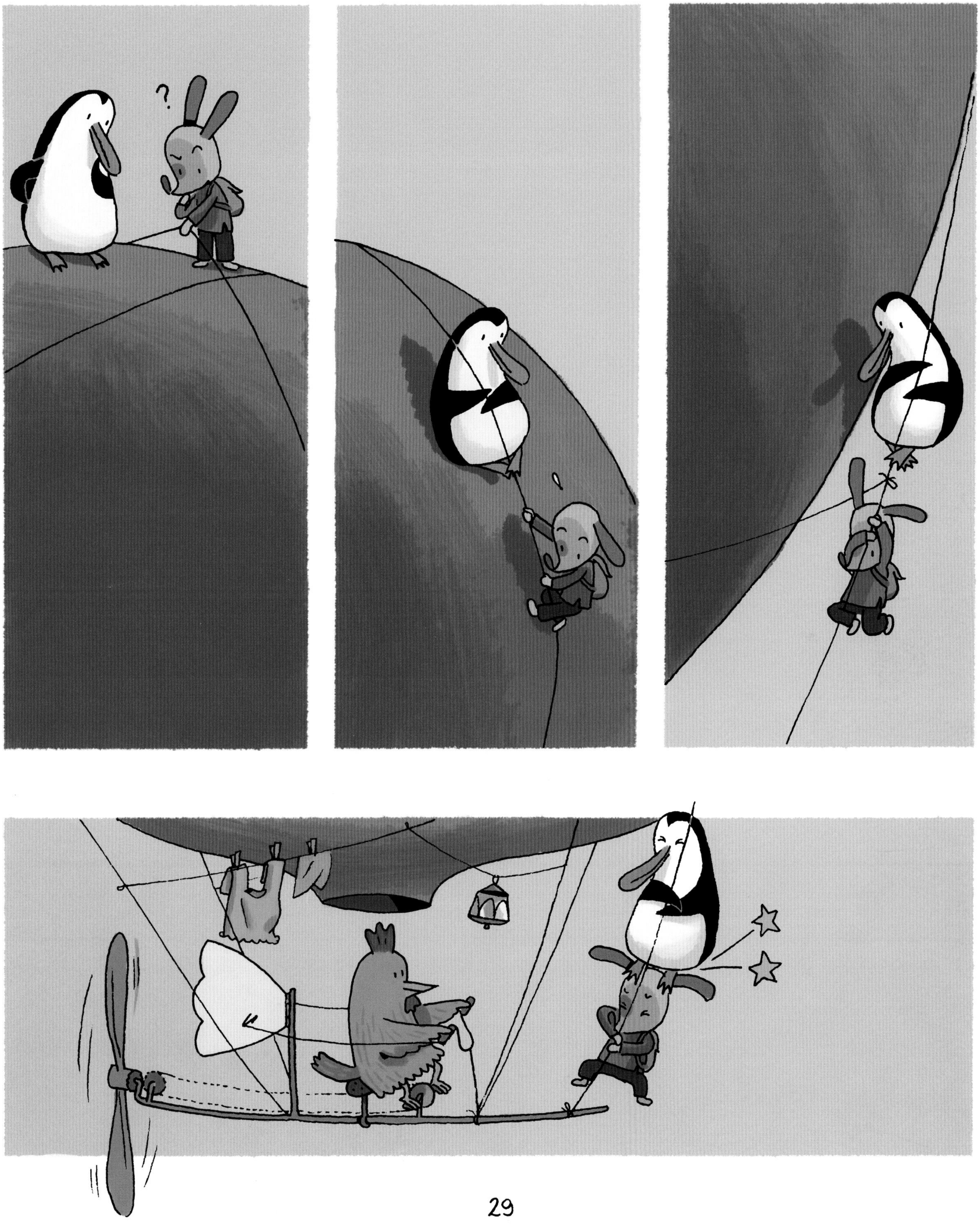
?
!

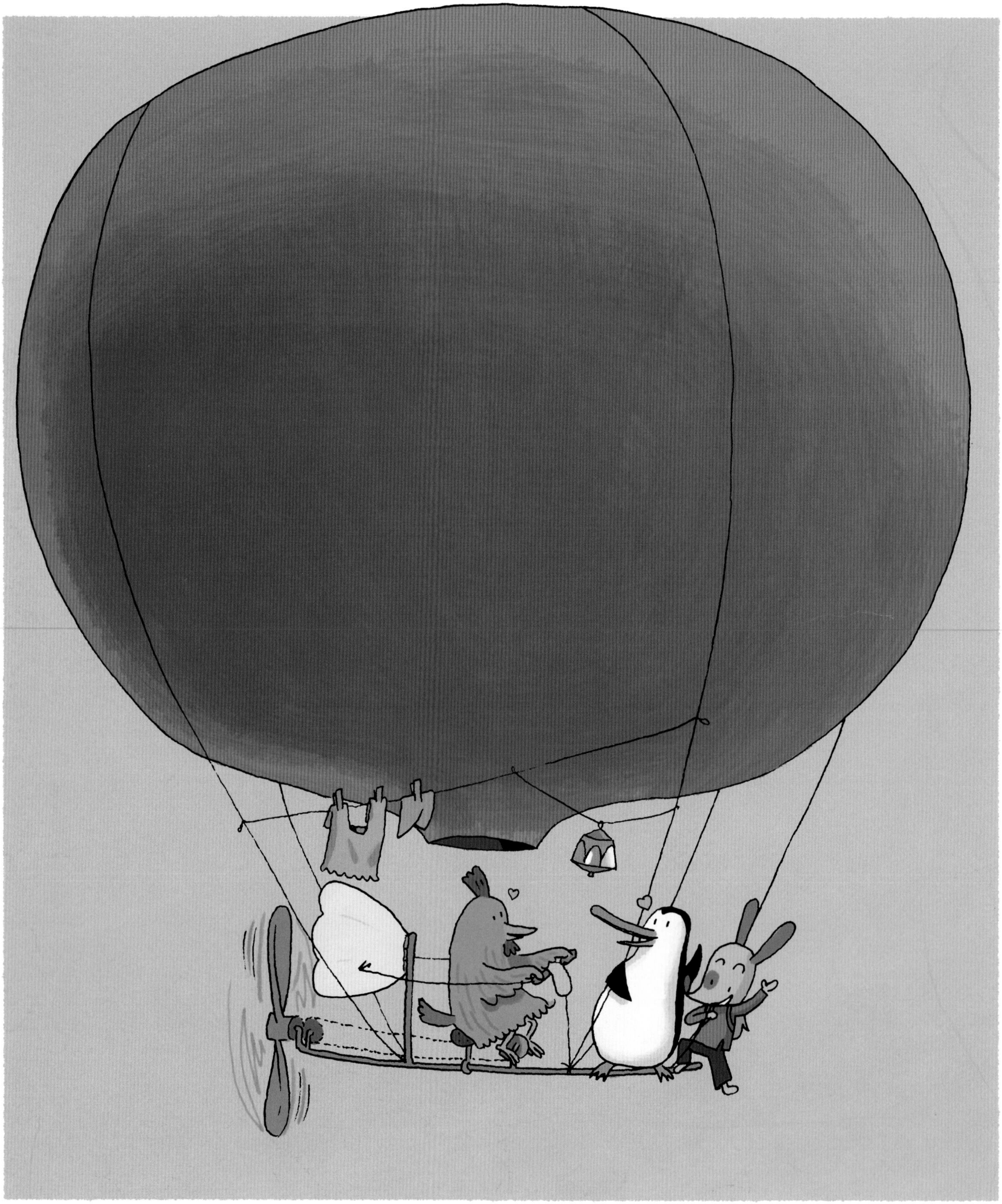

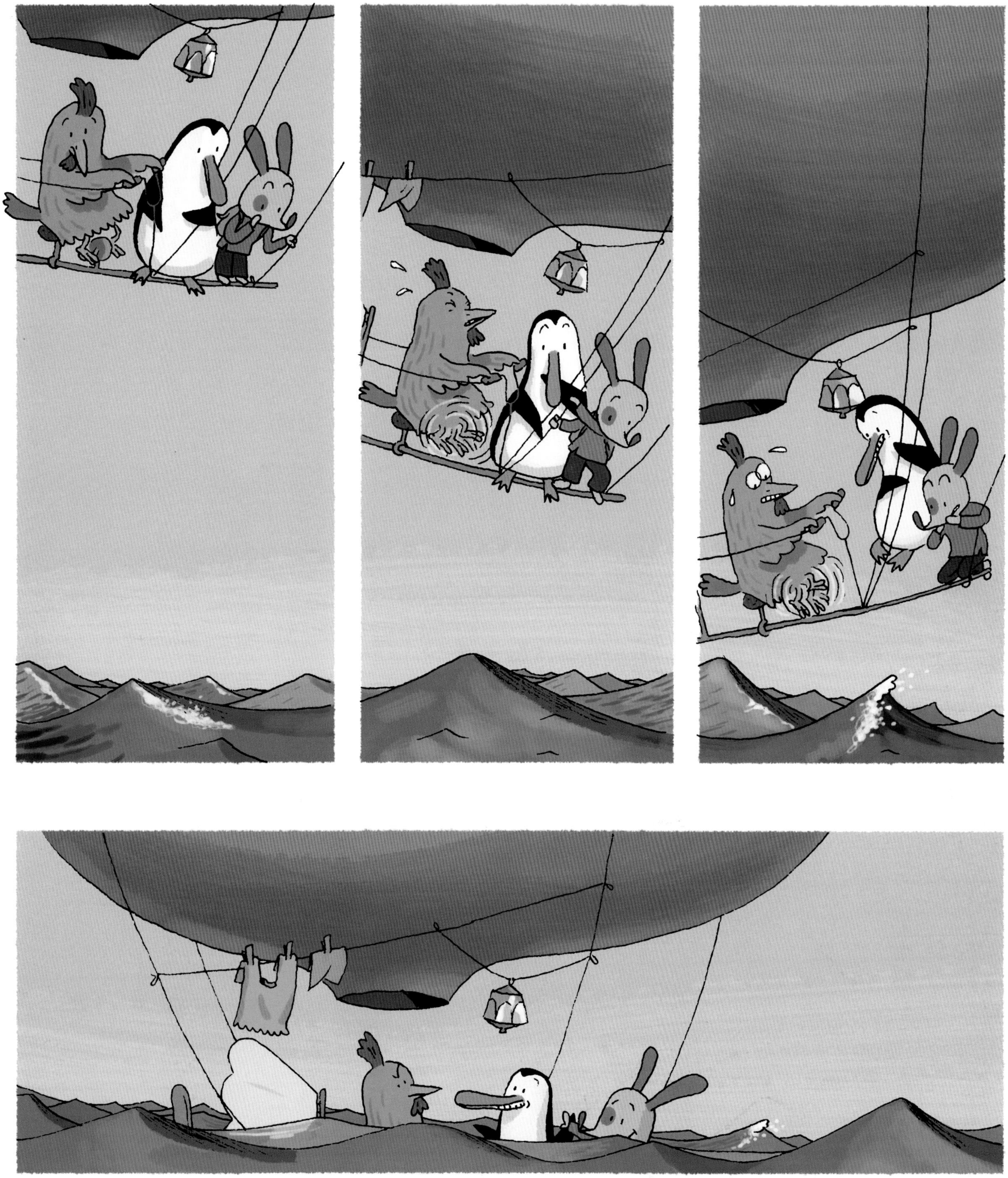

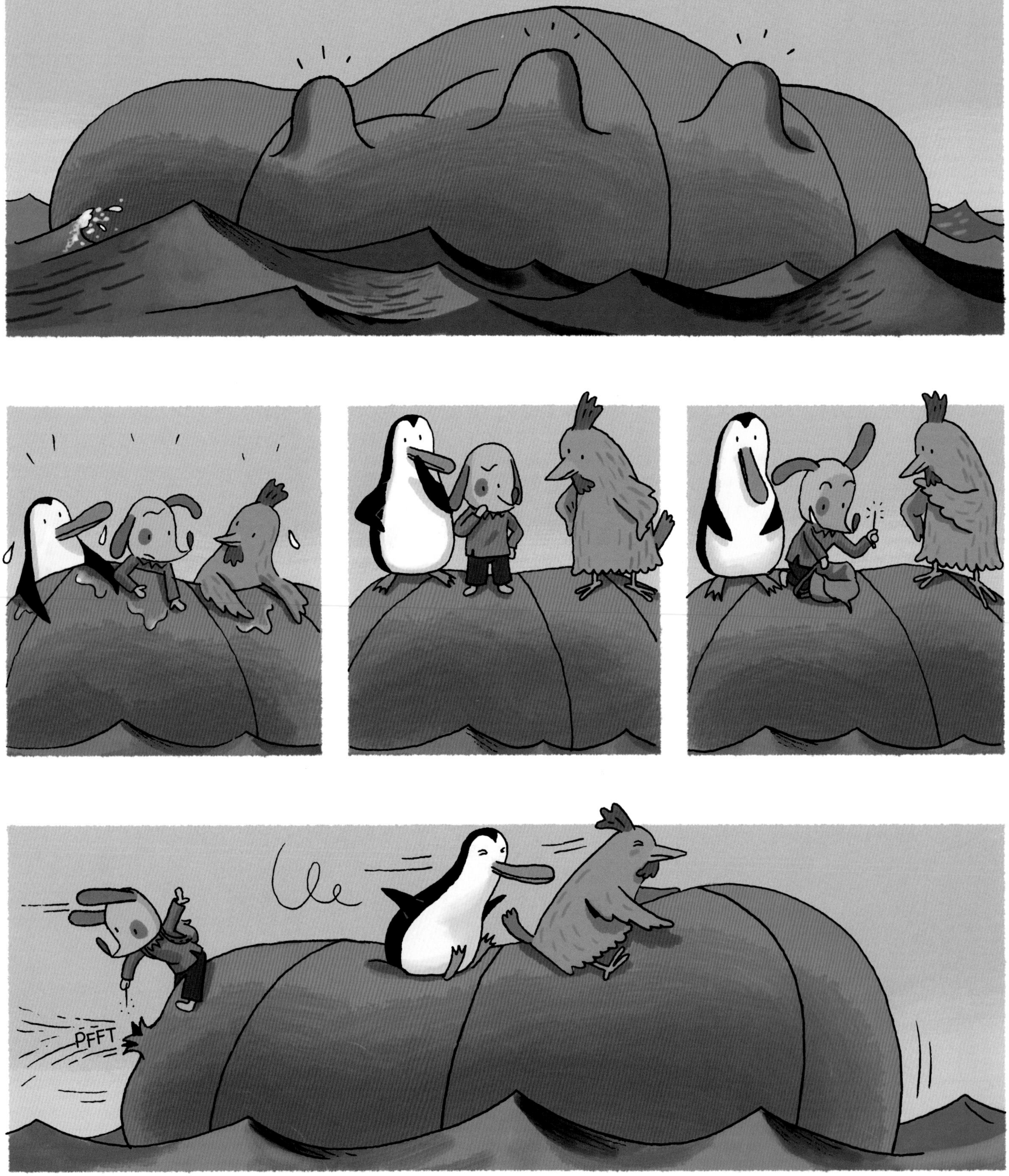
PFFT

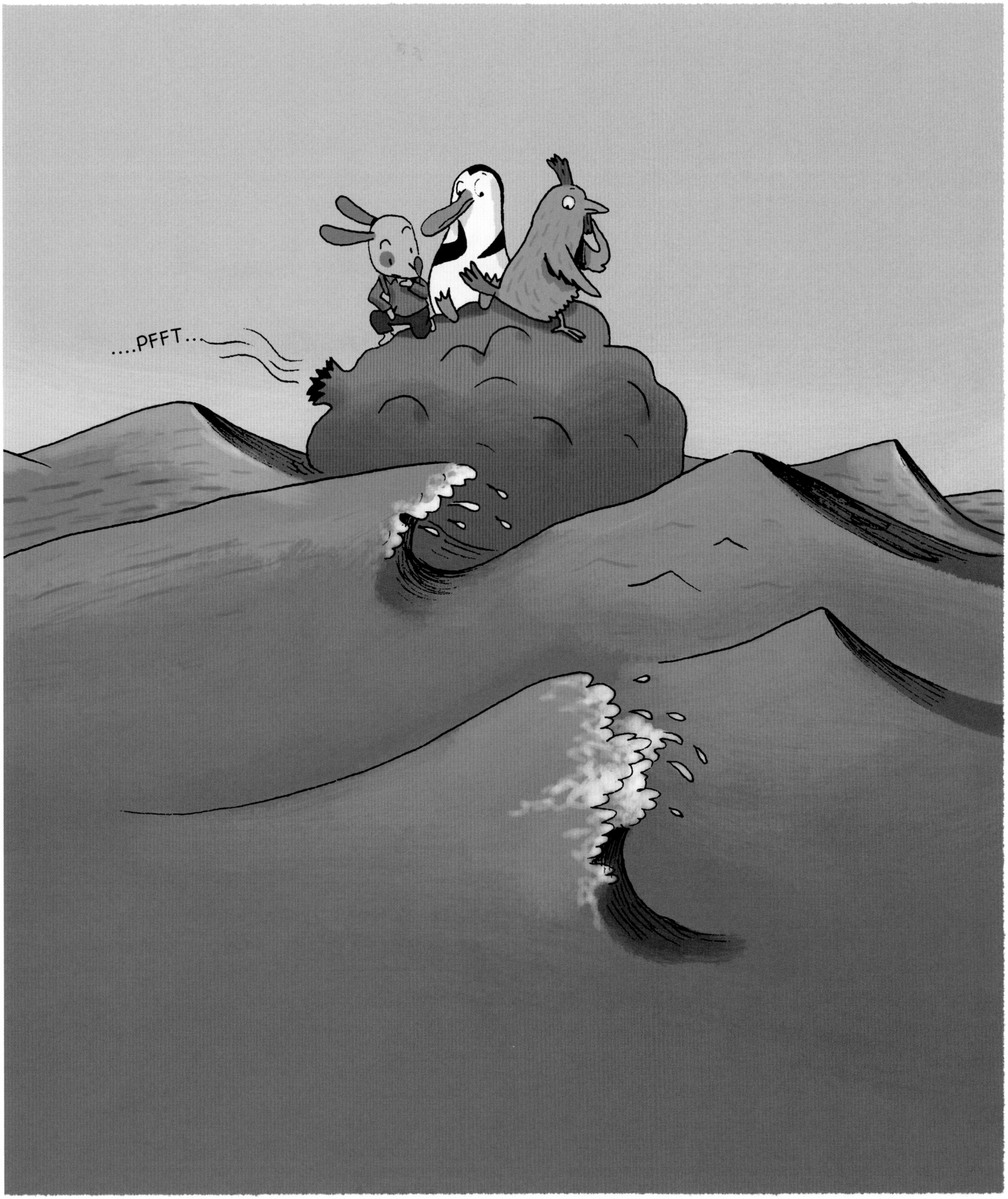
....PFFT...

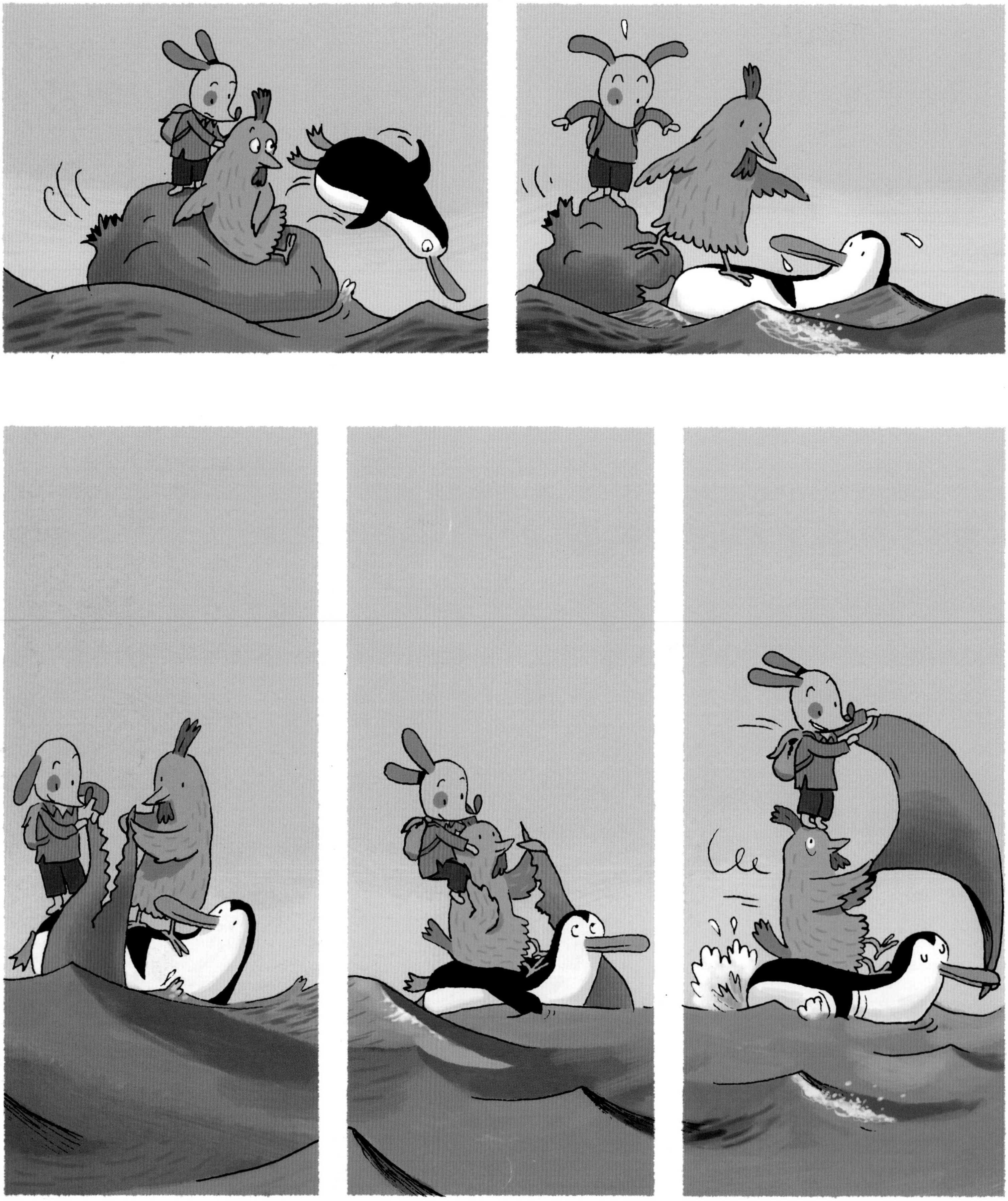

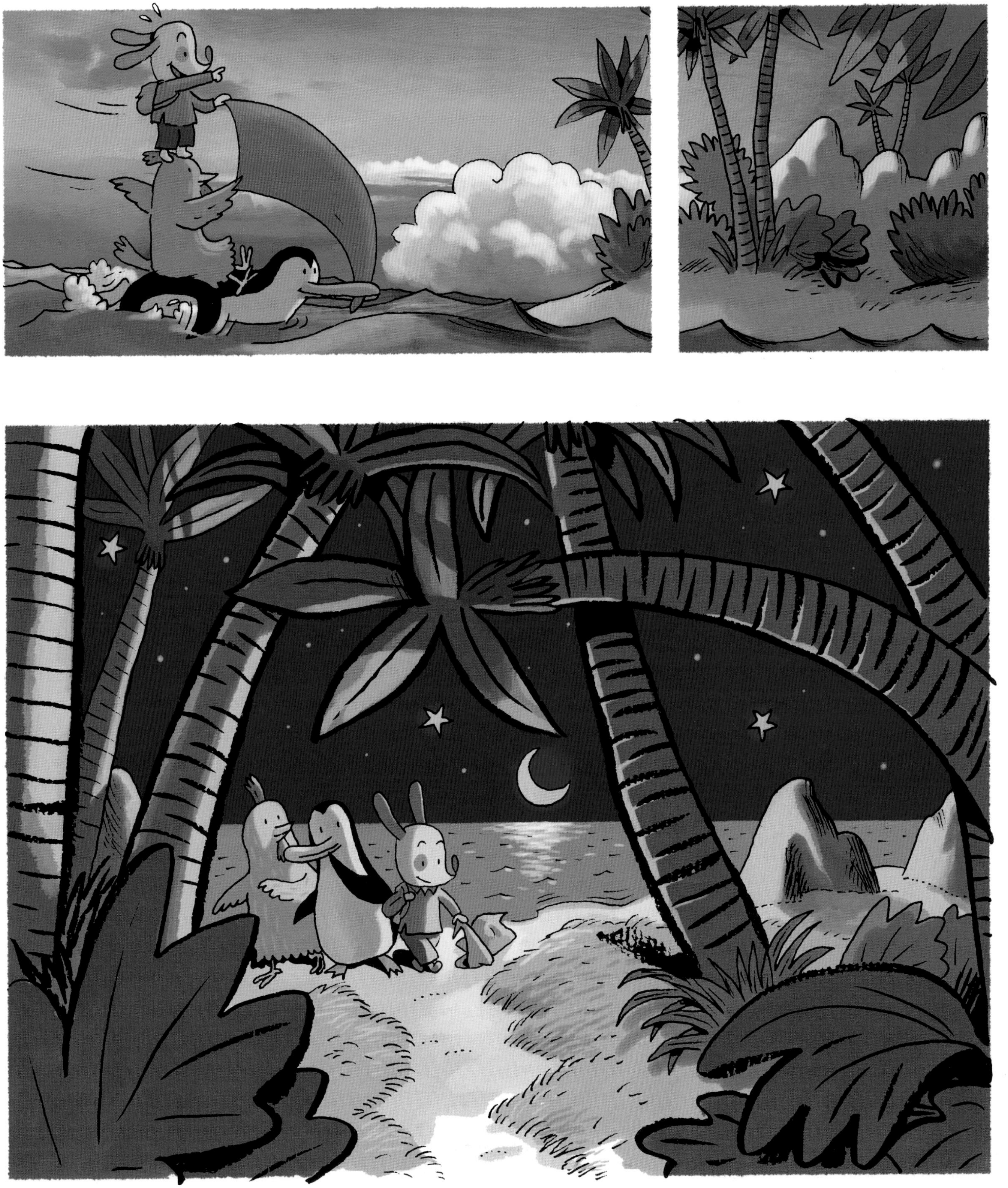

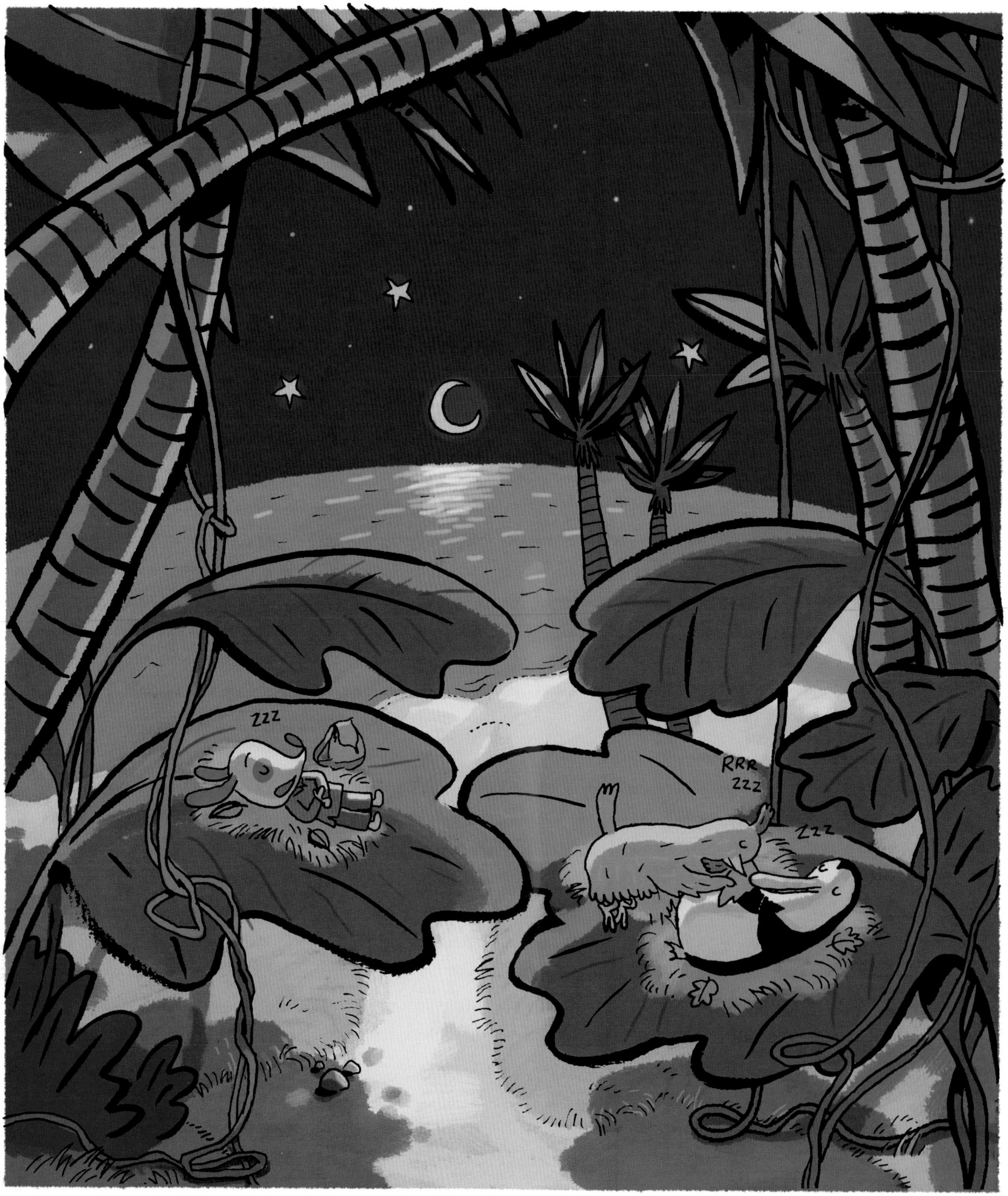
ZZZ
RRR
ZZZ
ZZZ

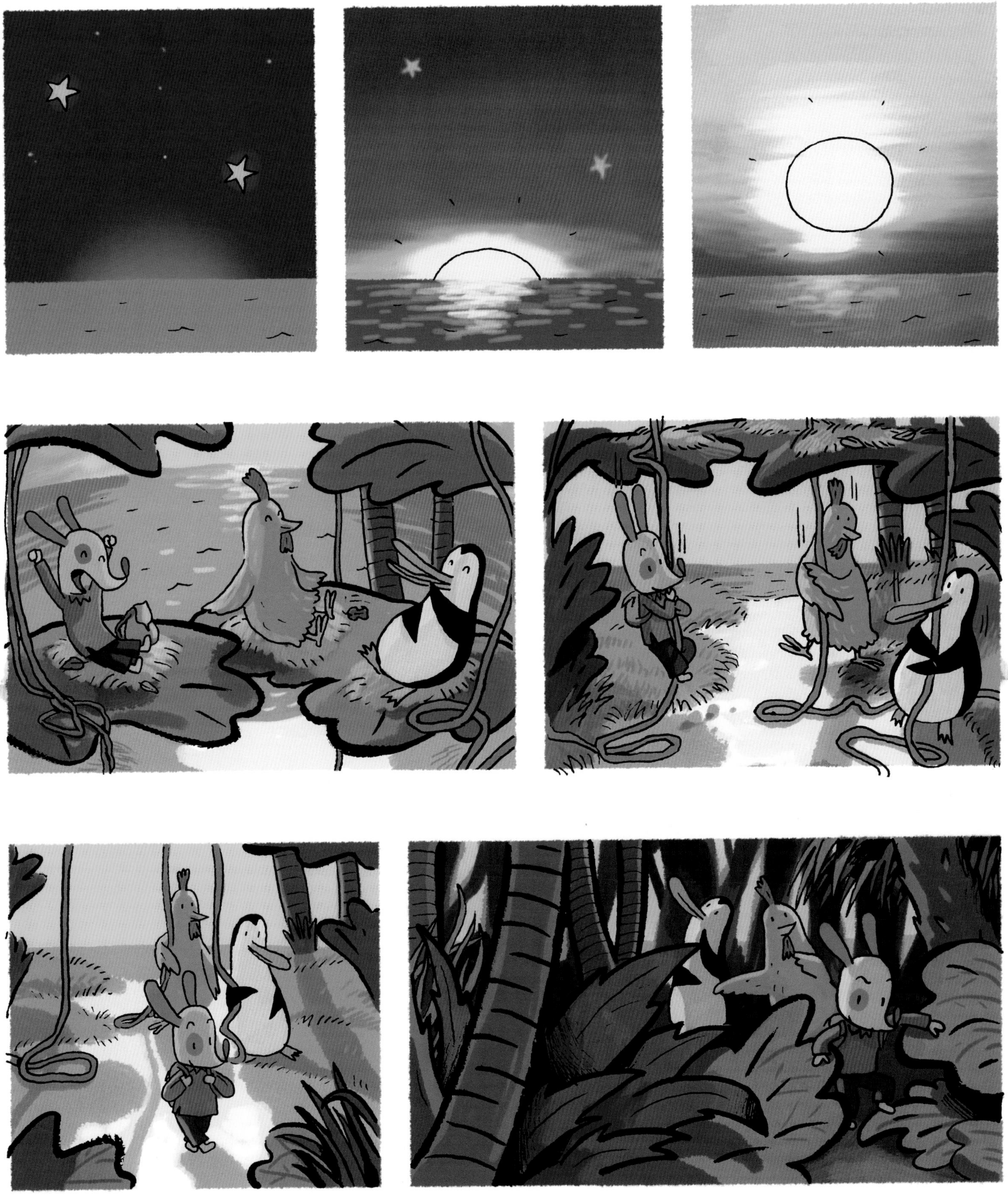

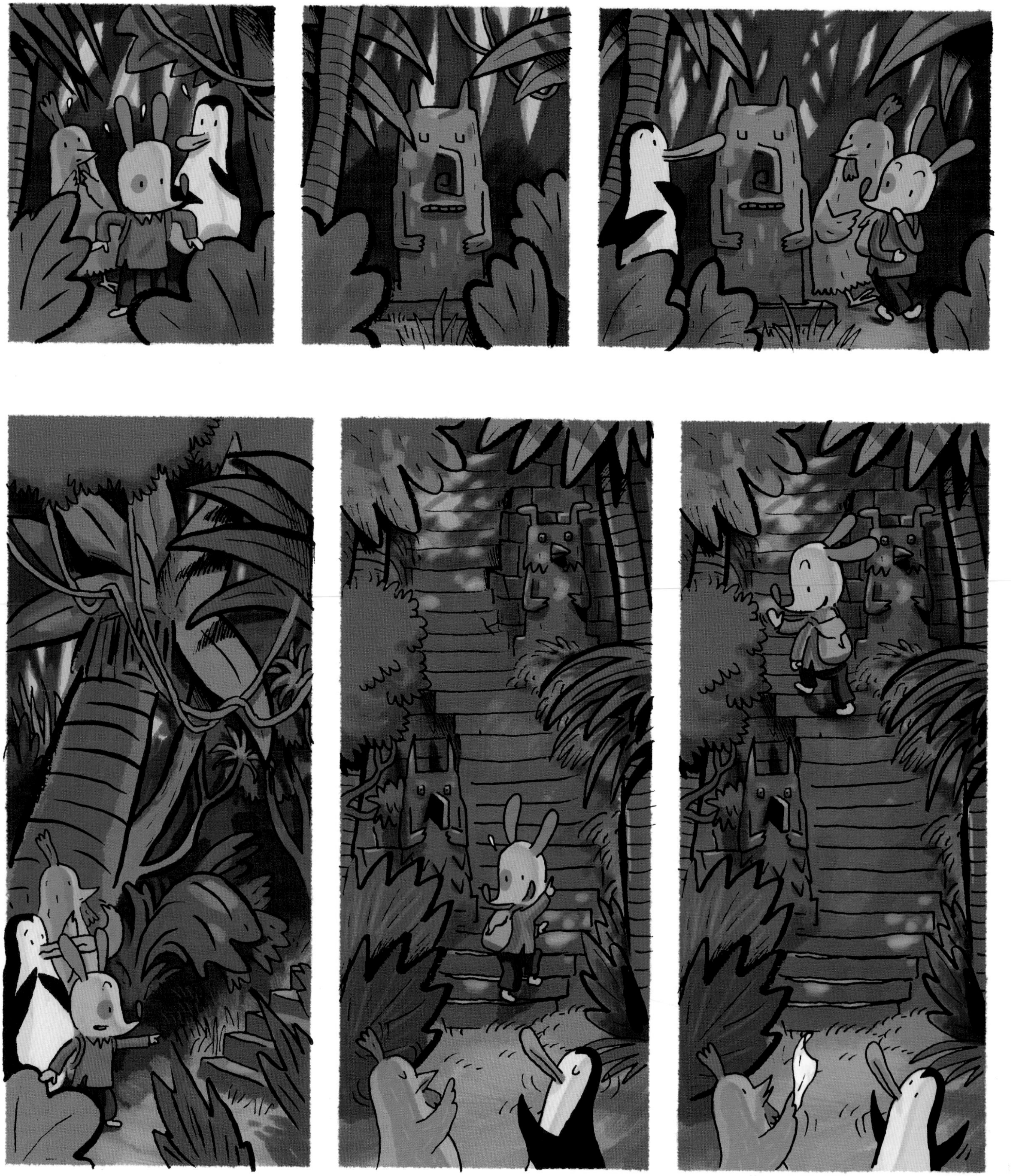

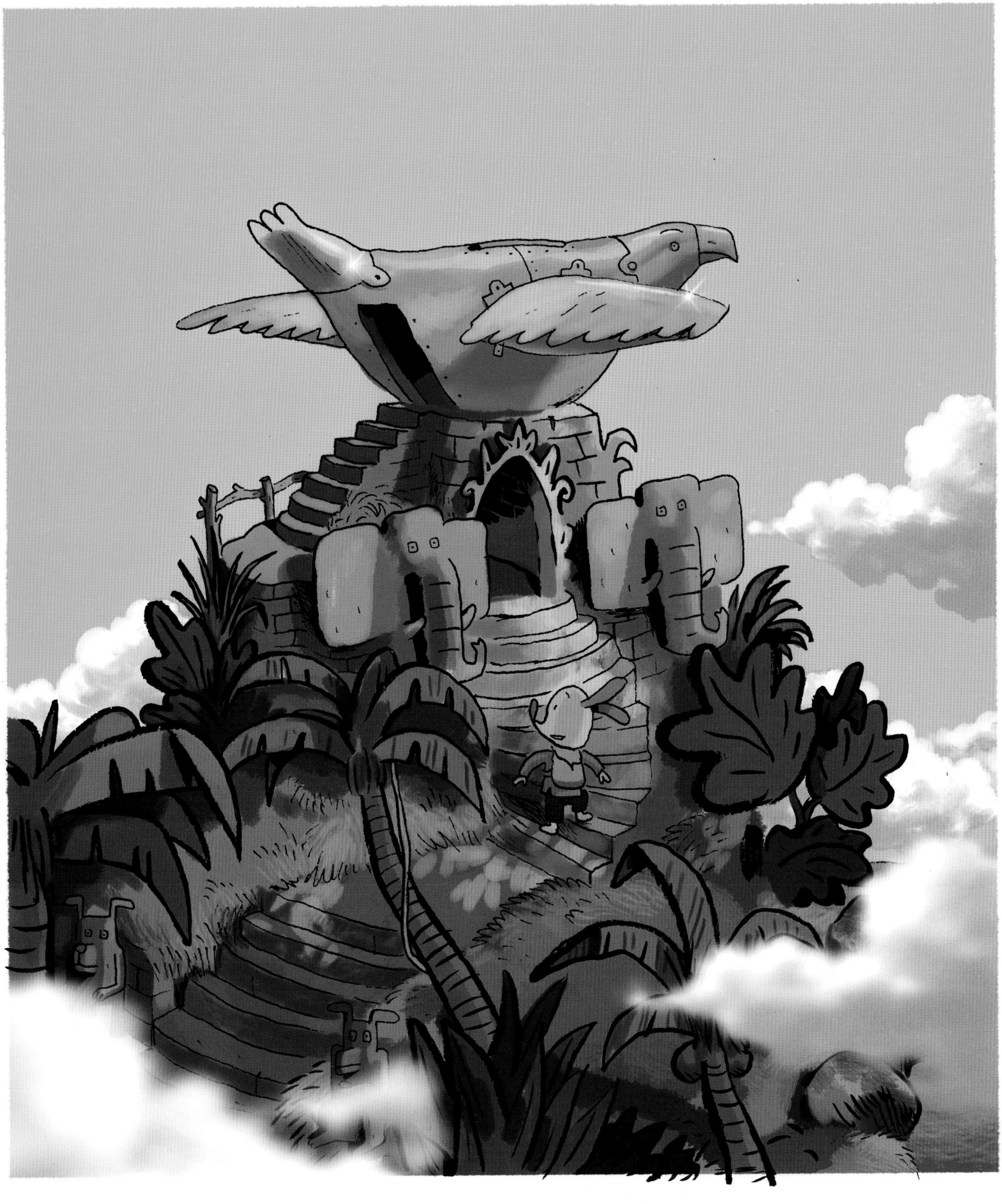

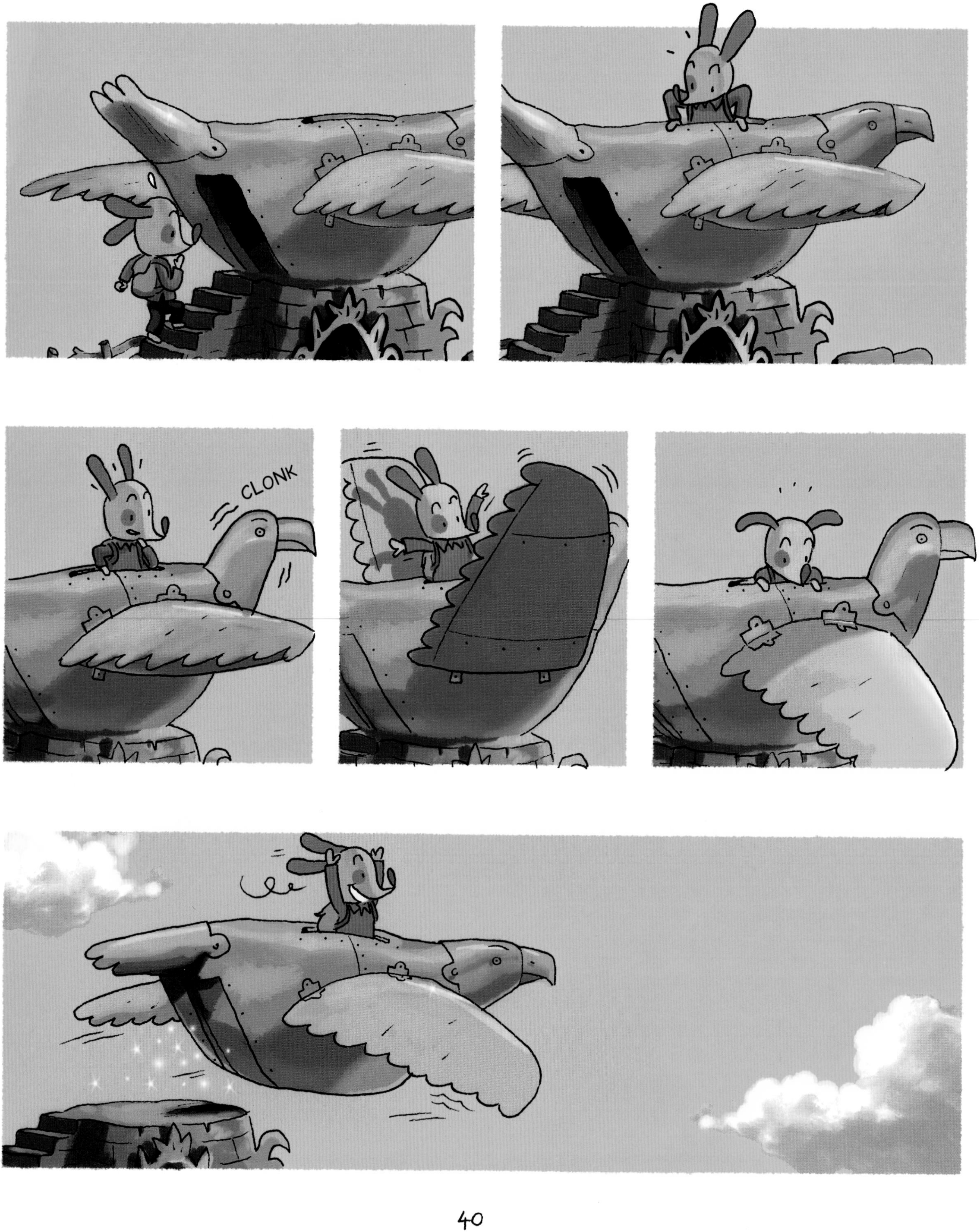
CLONK

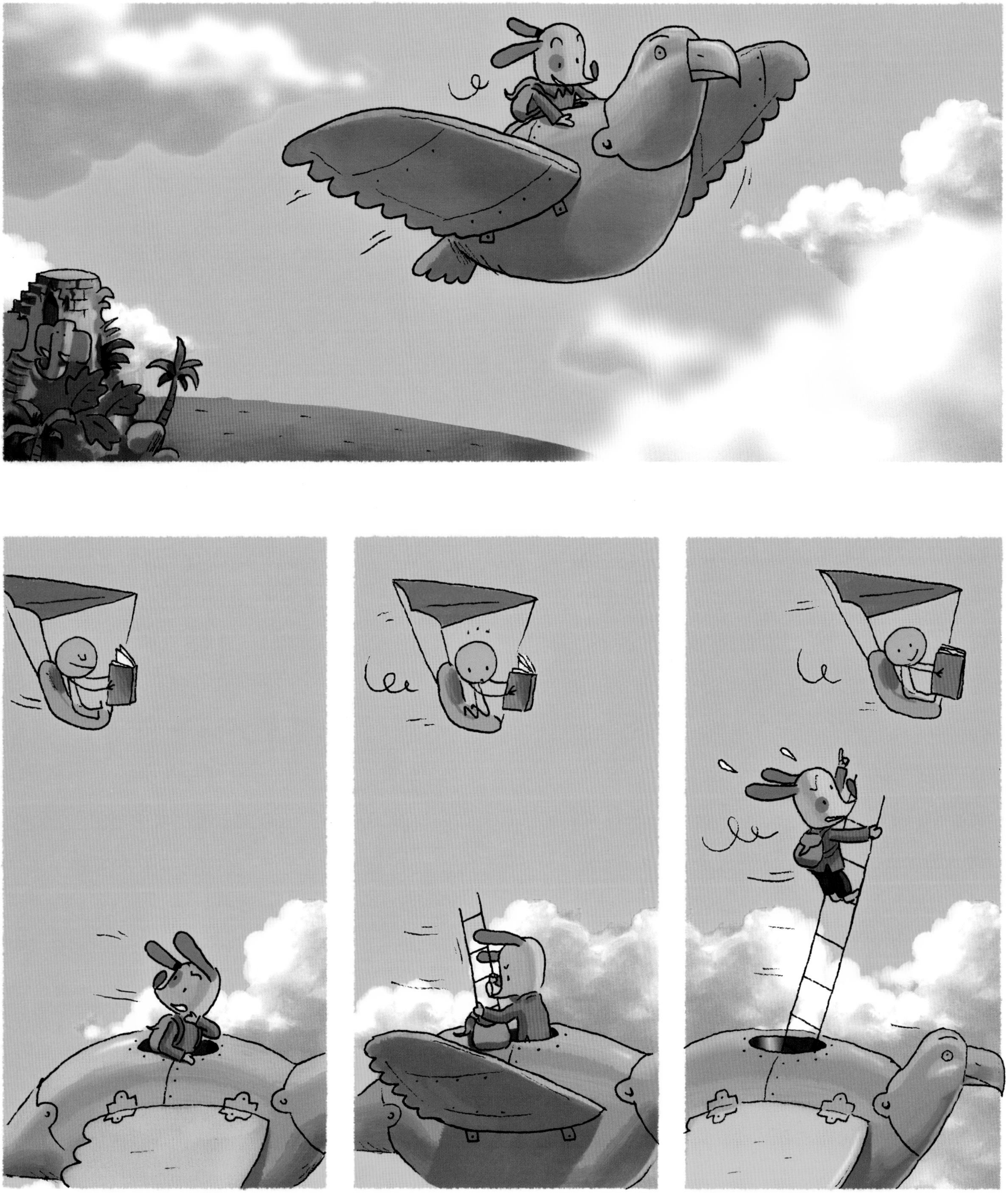

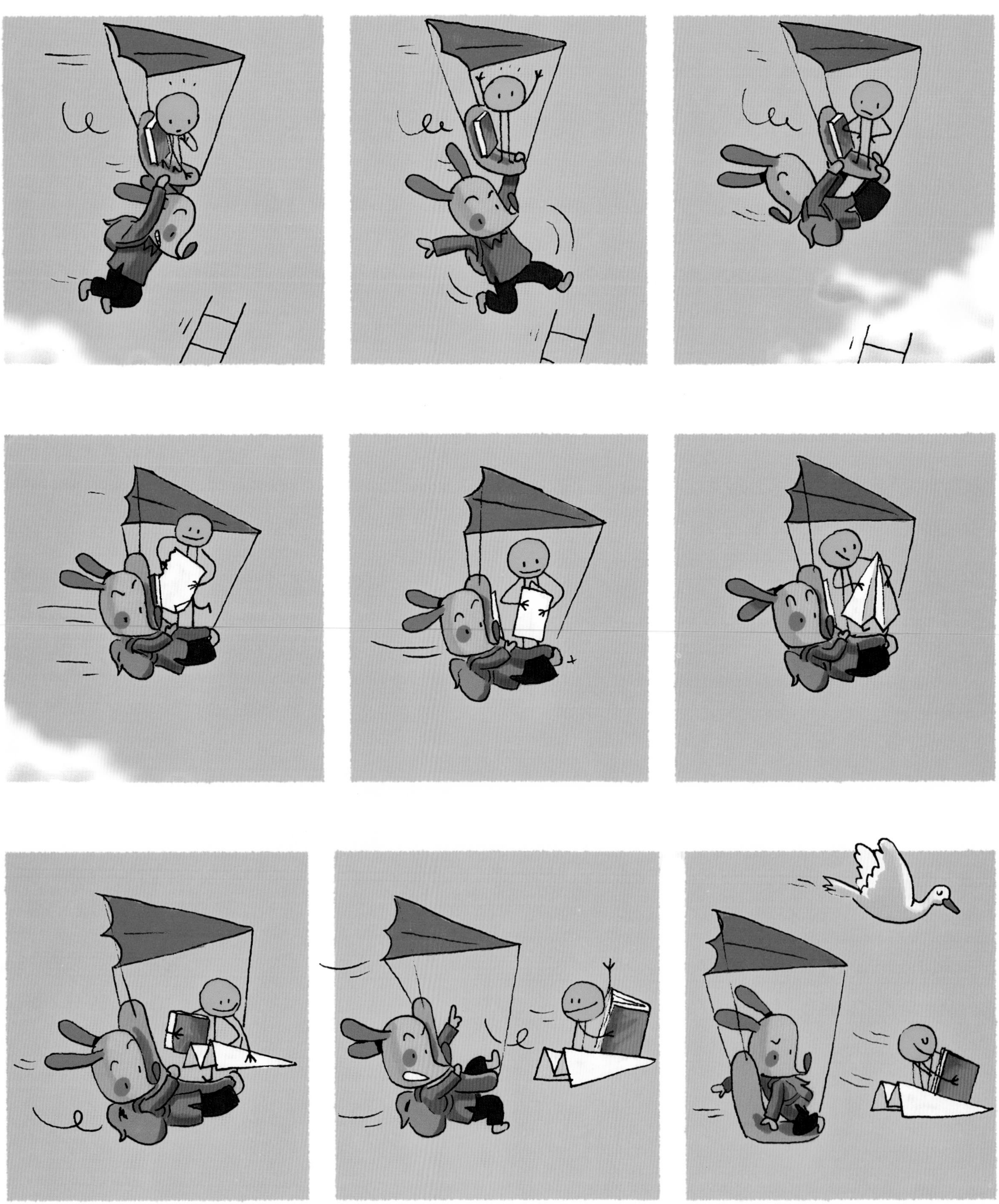

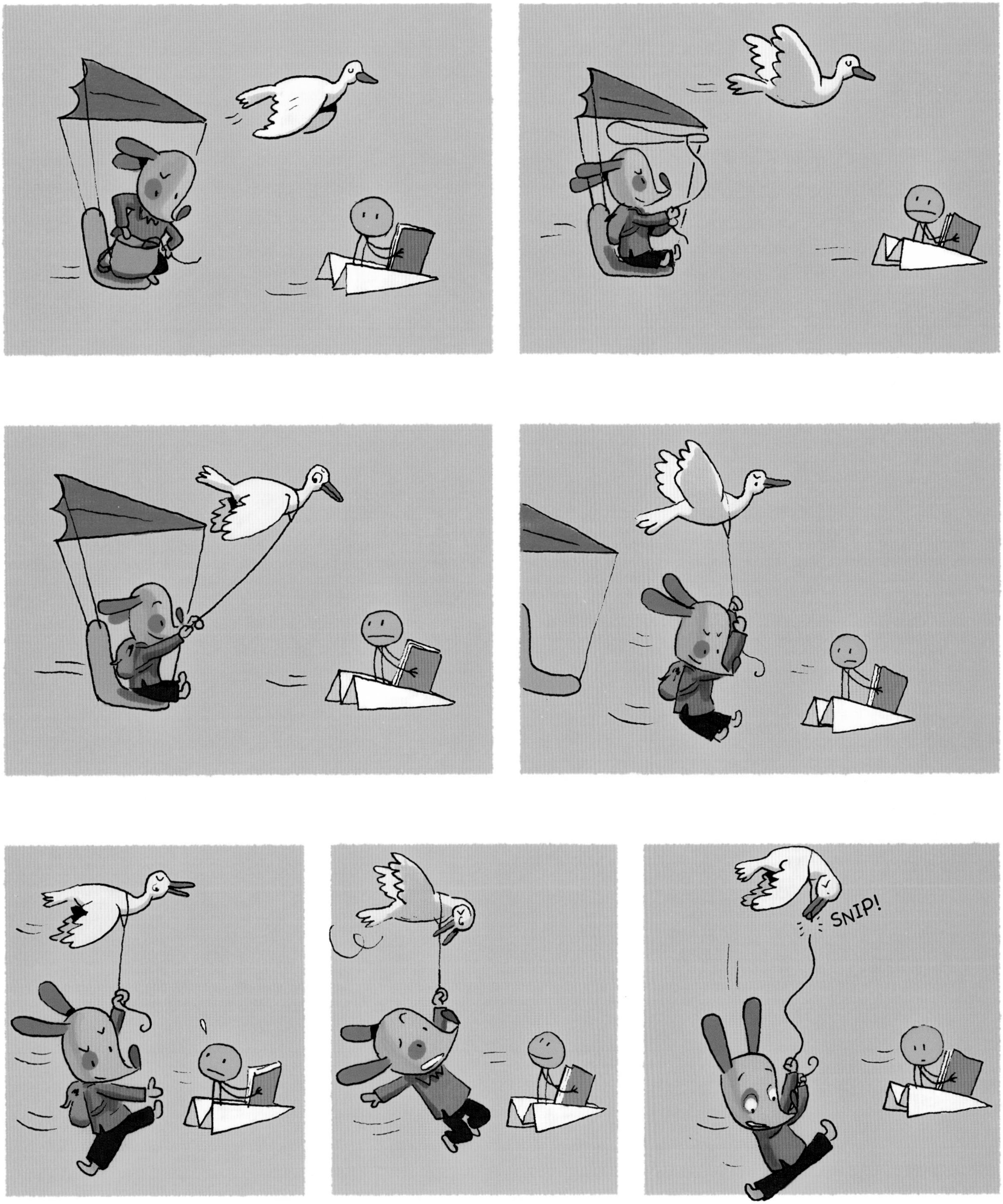
SNIP!

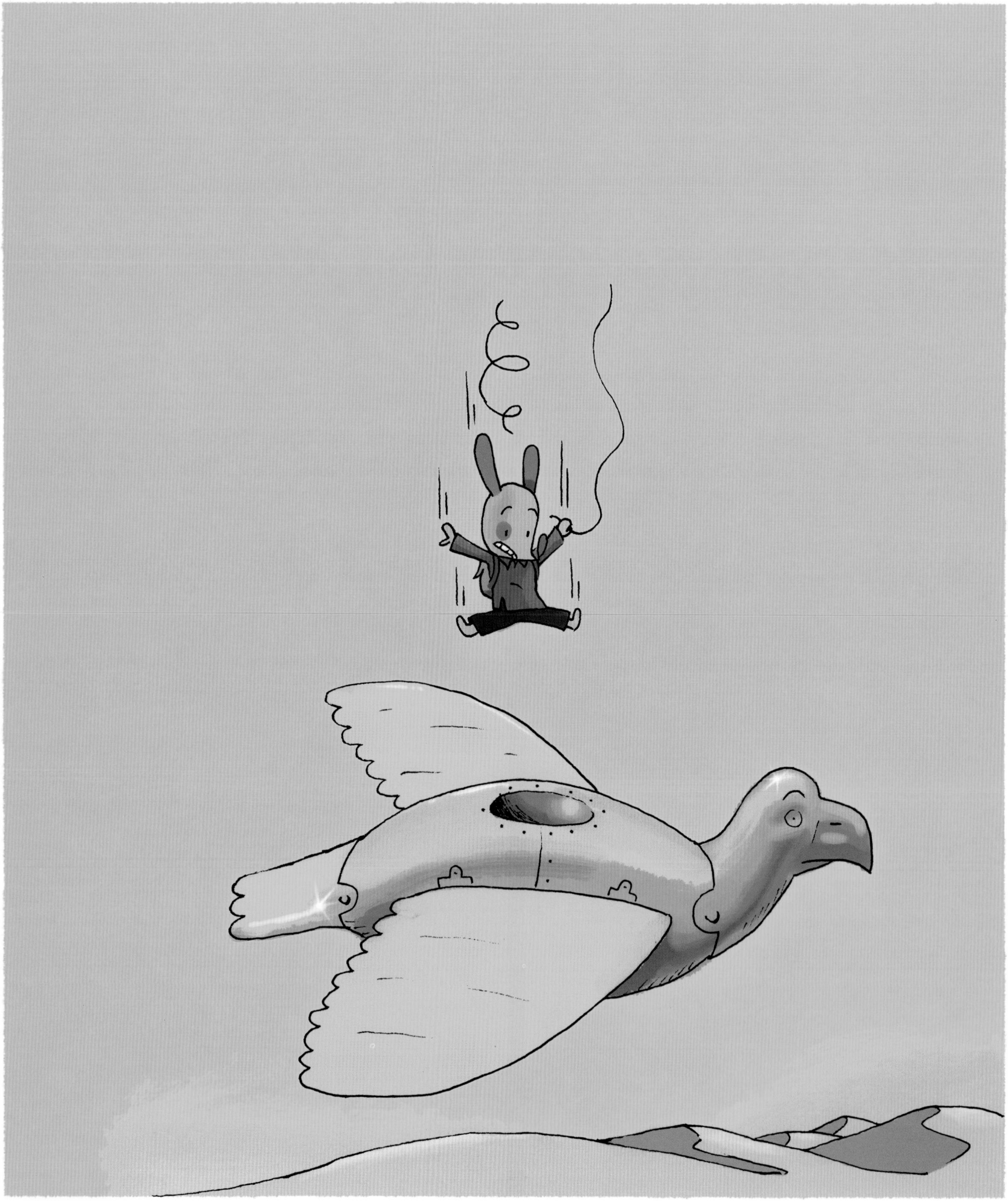

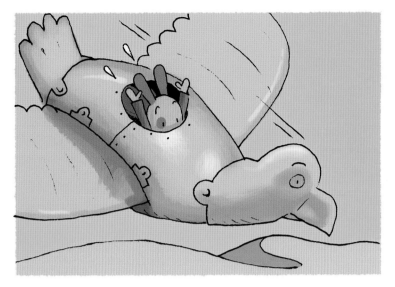

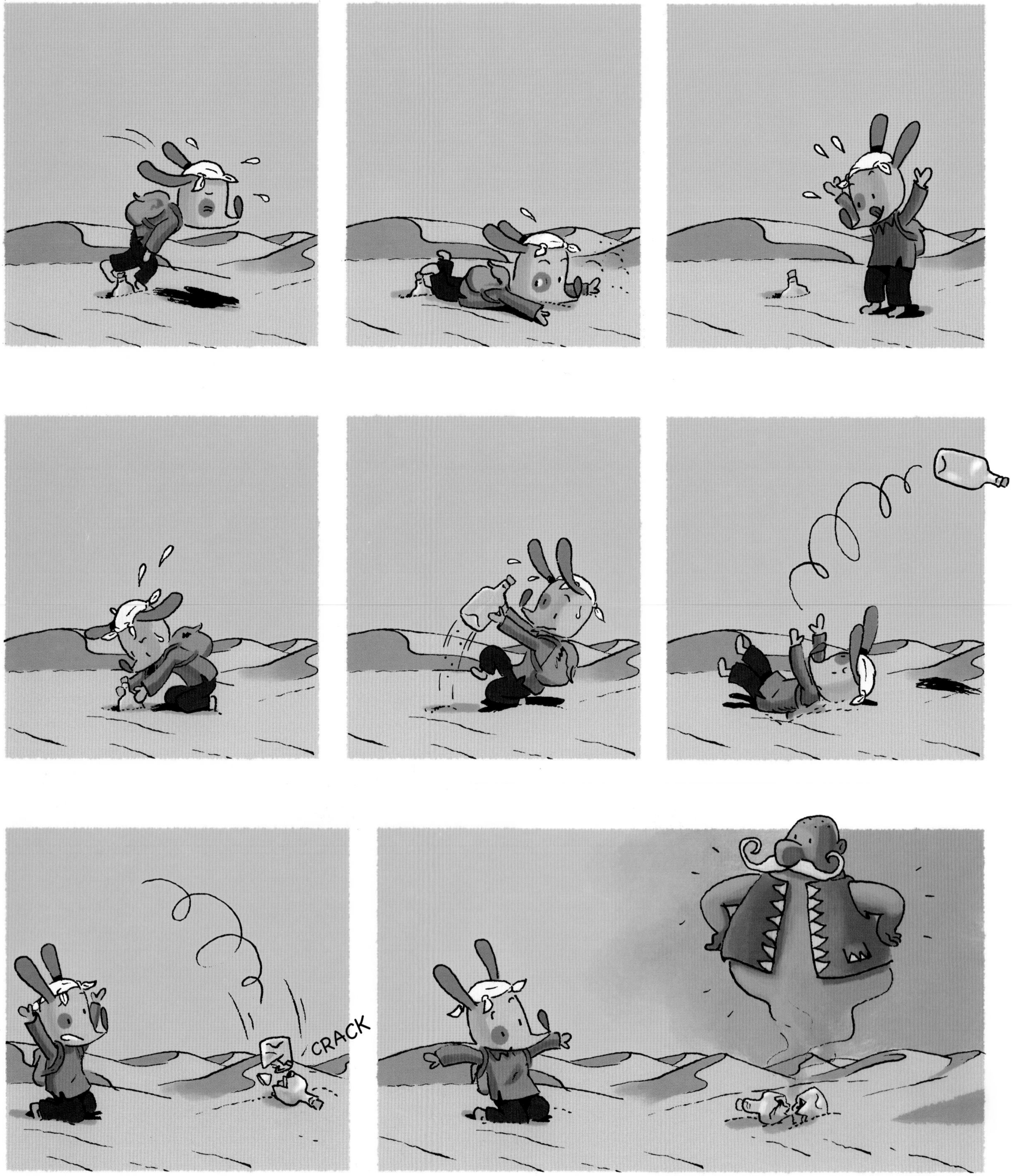
CRACK

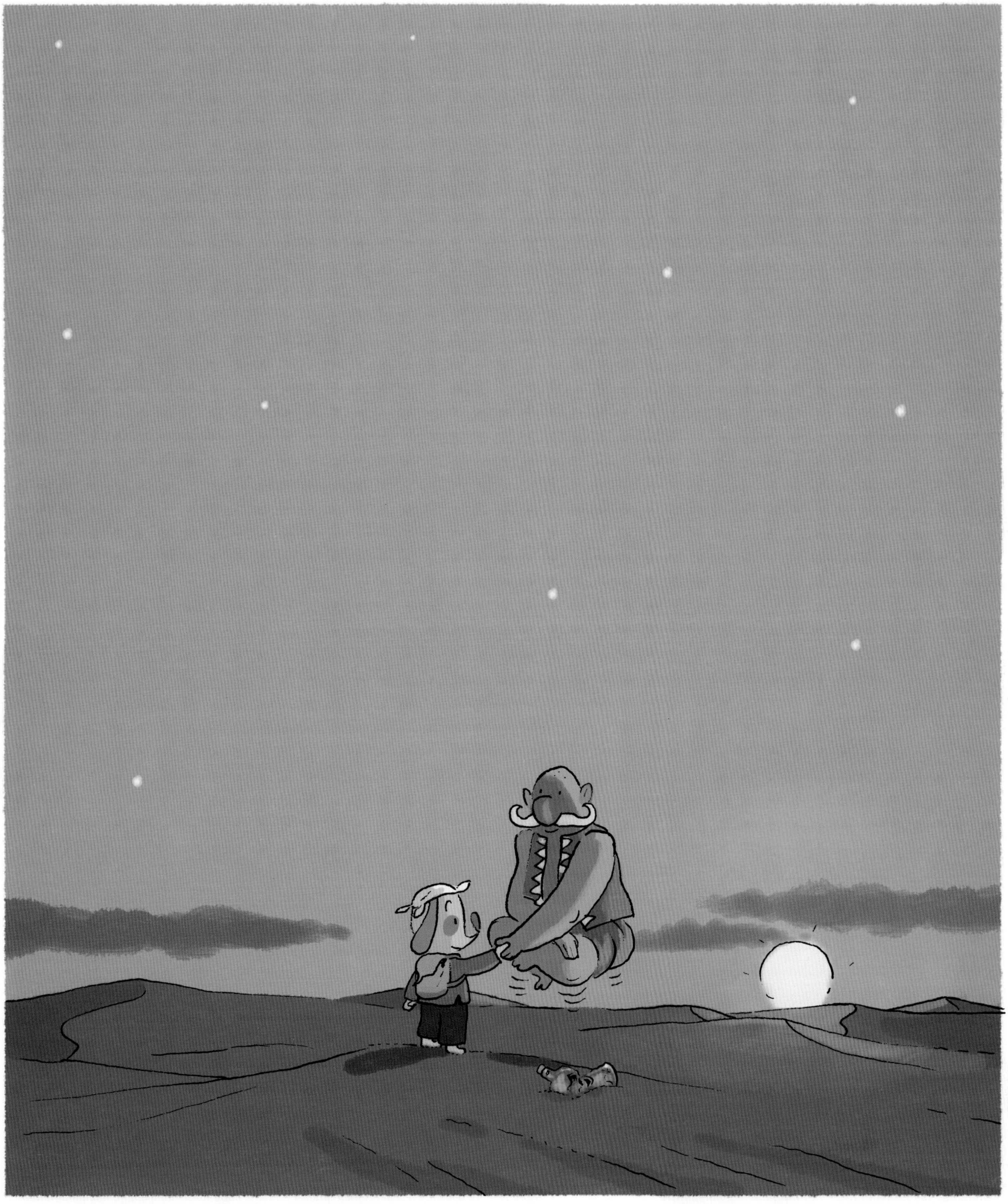

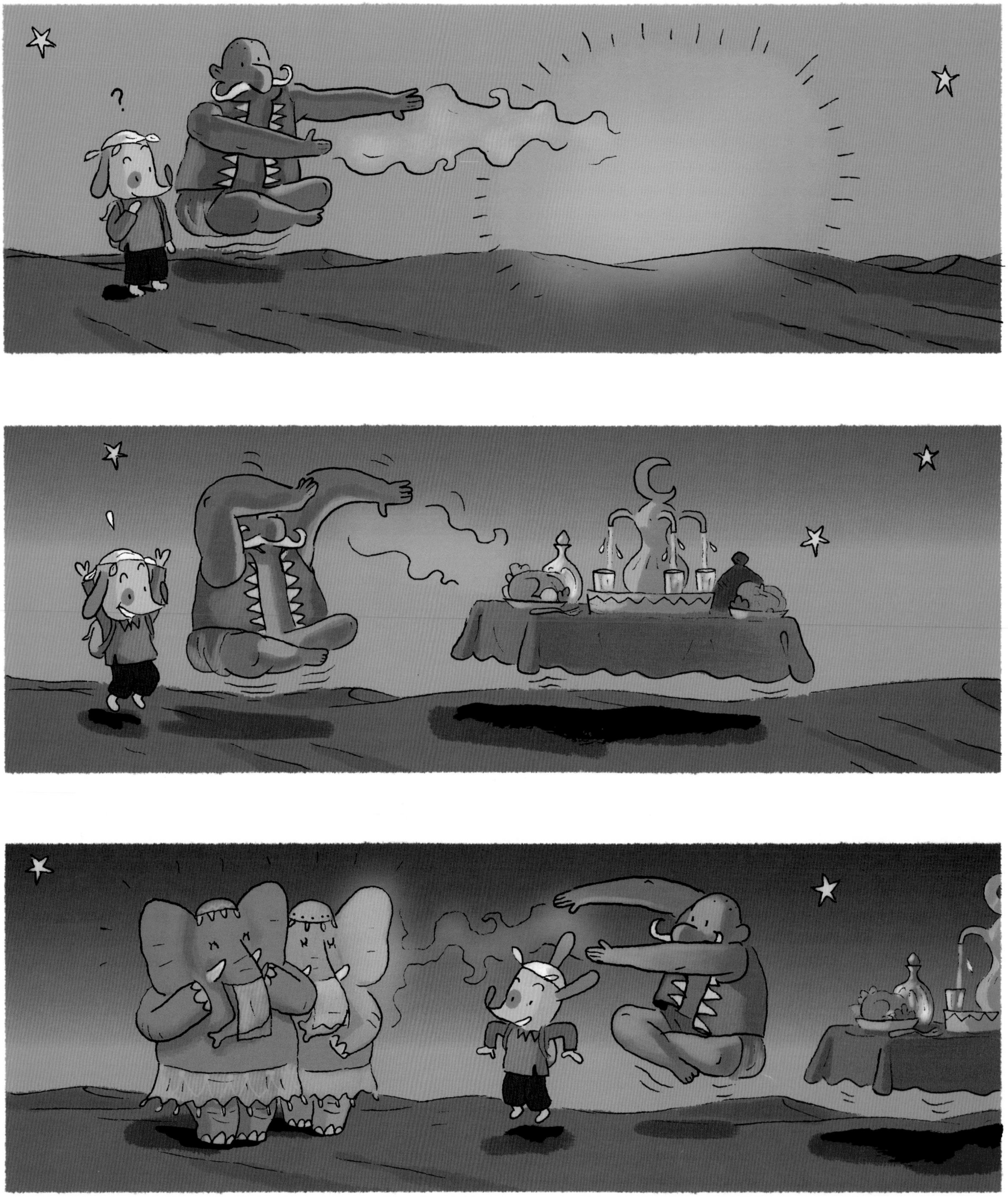

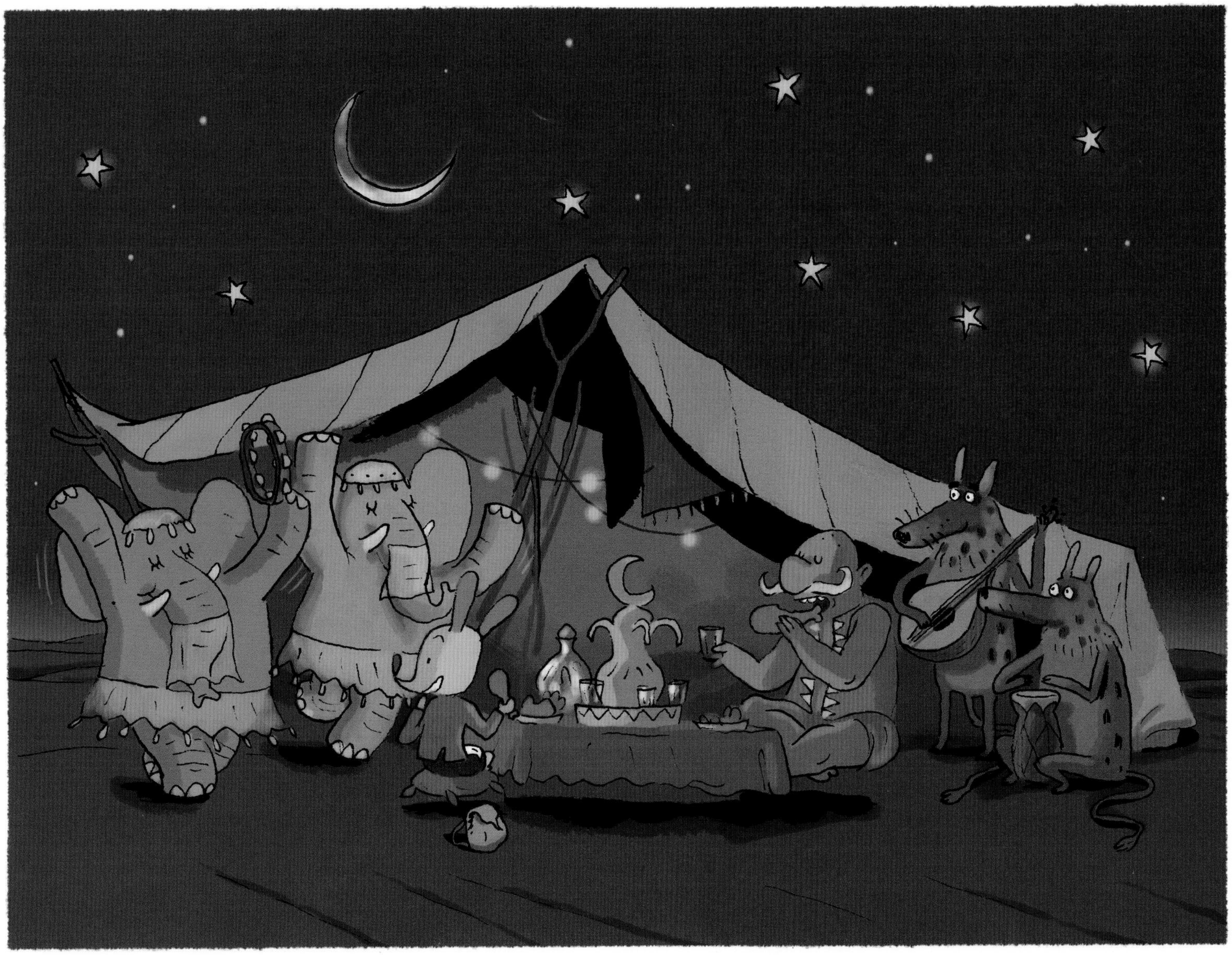

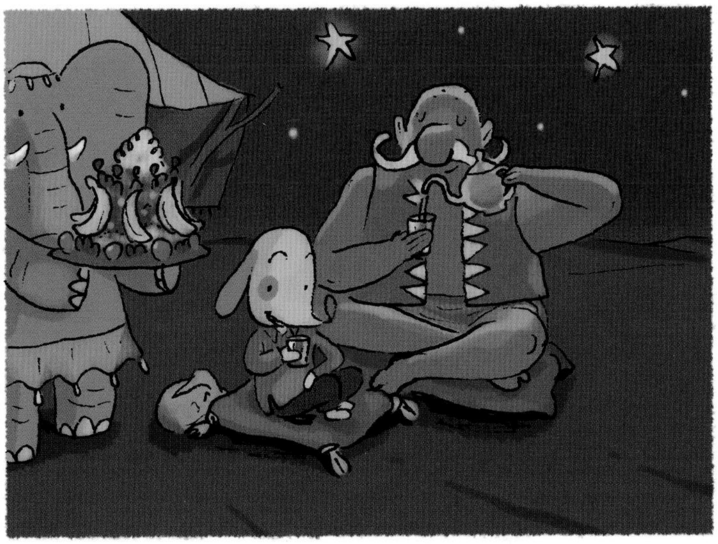

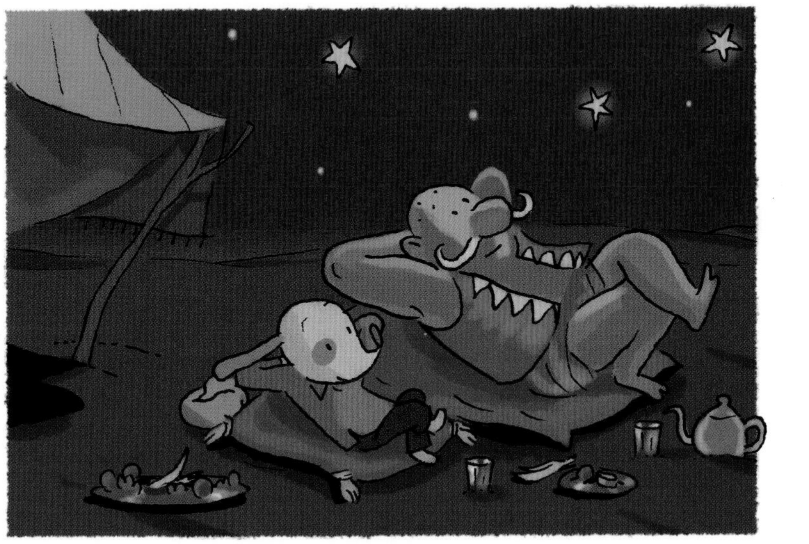

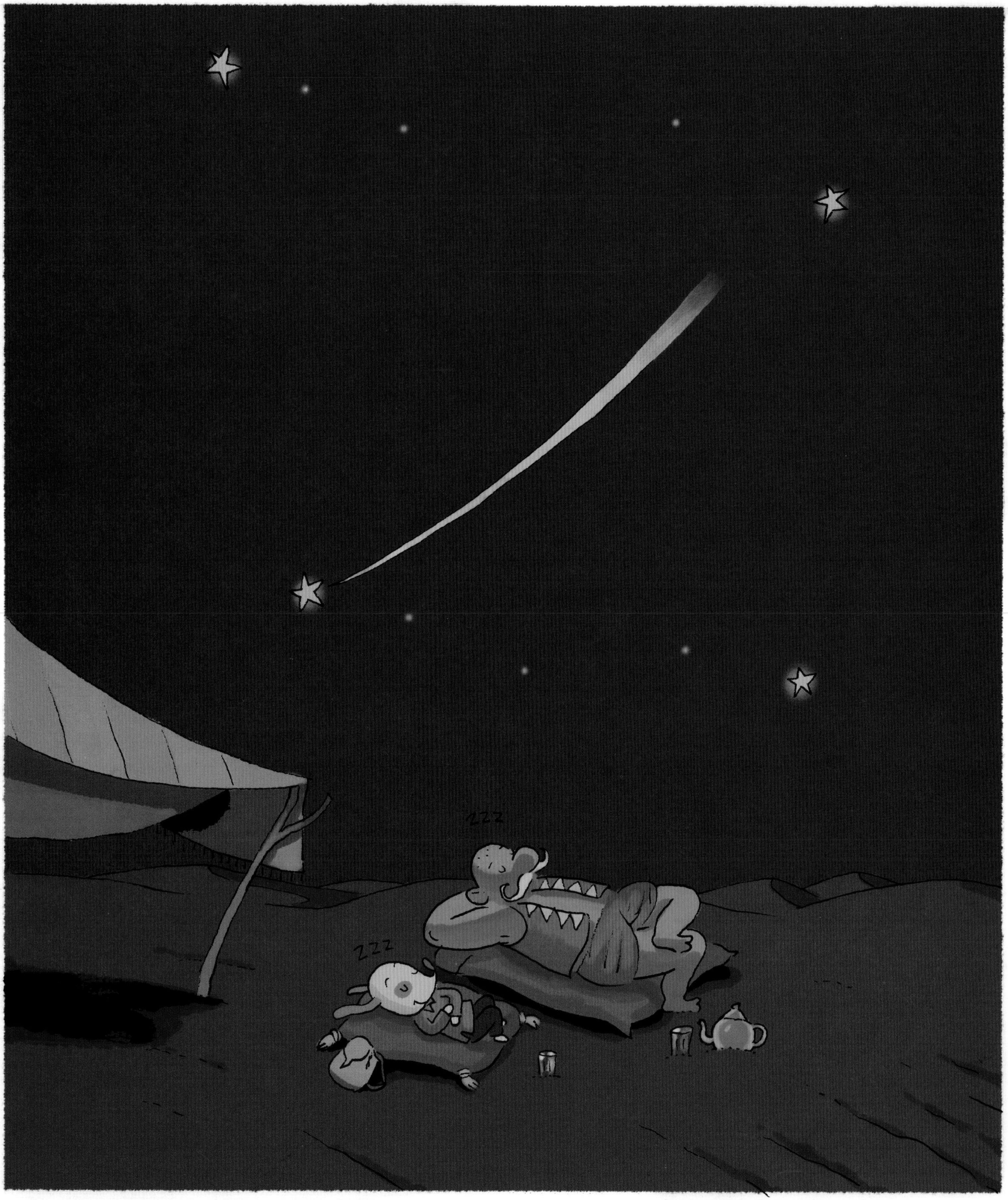
zzz
zzz

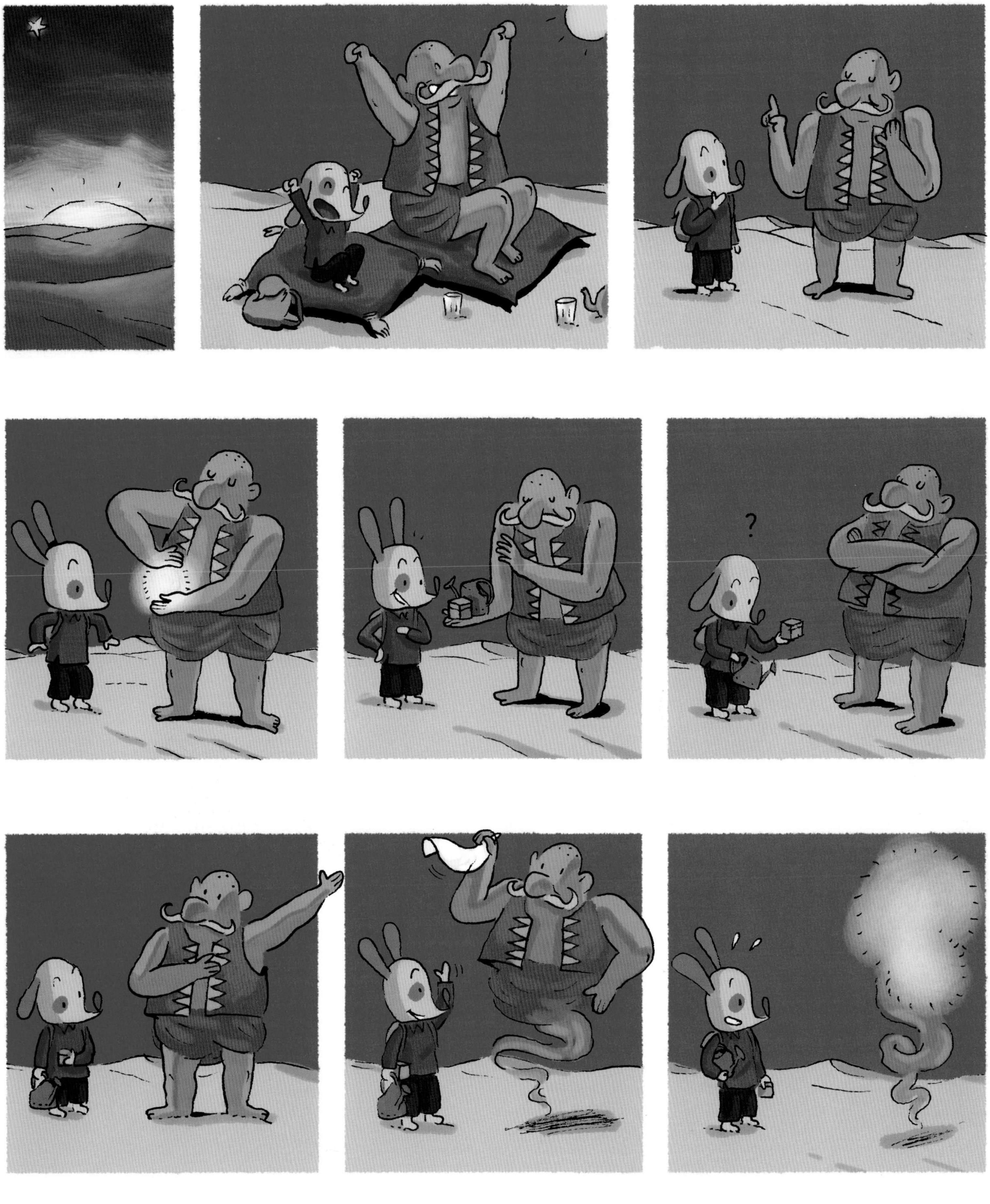
?

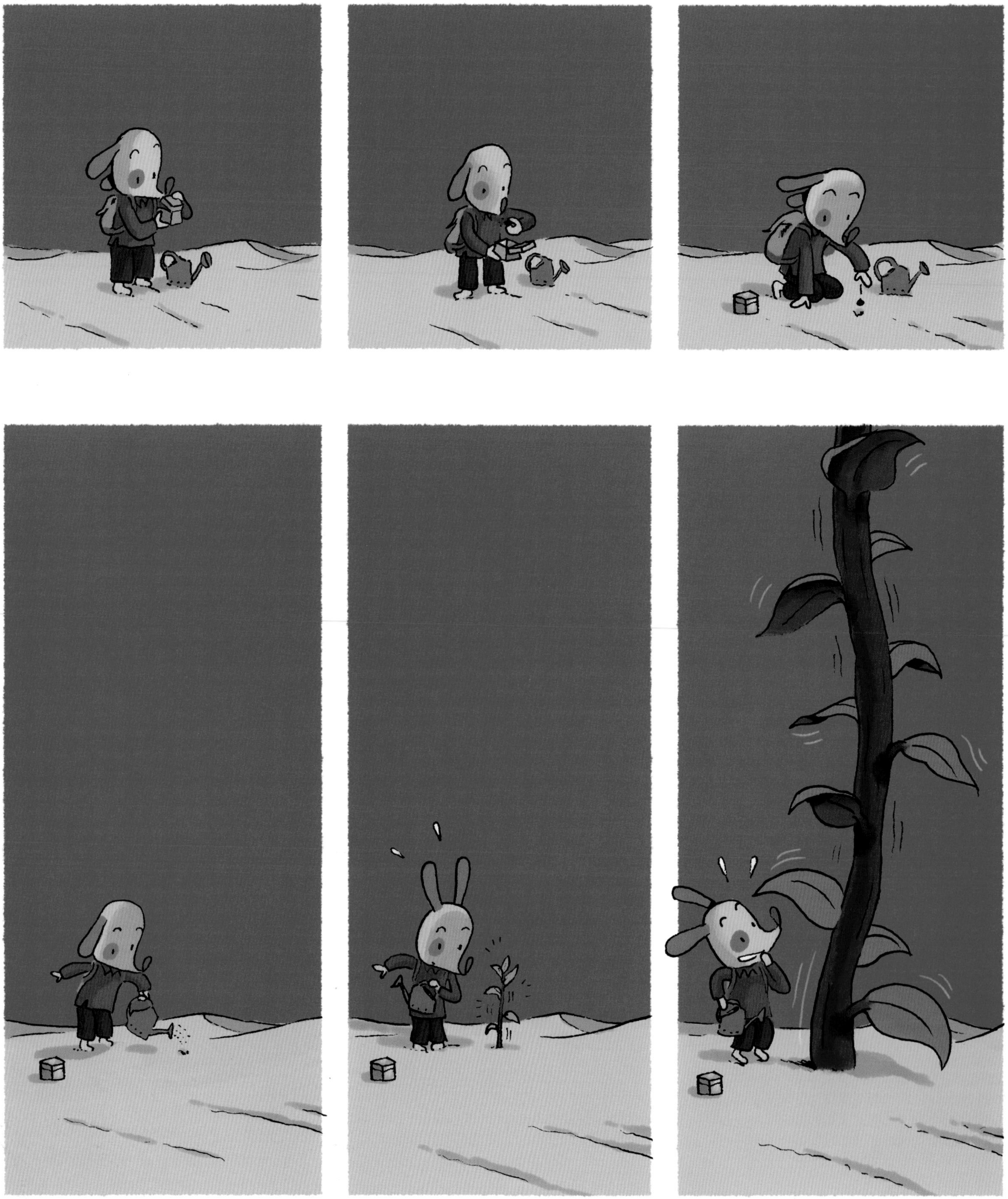

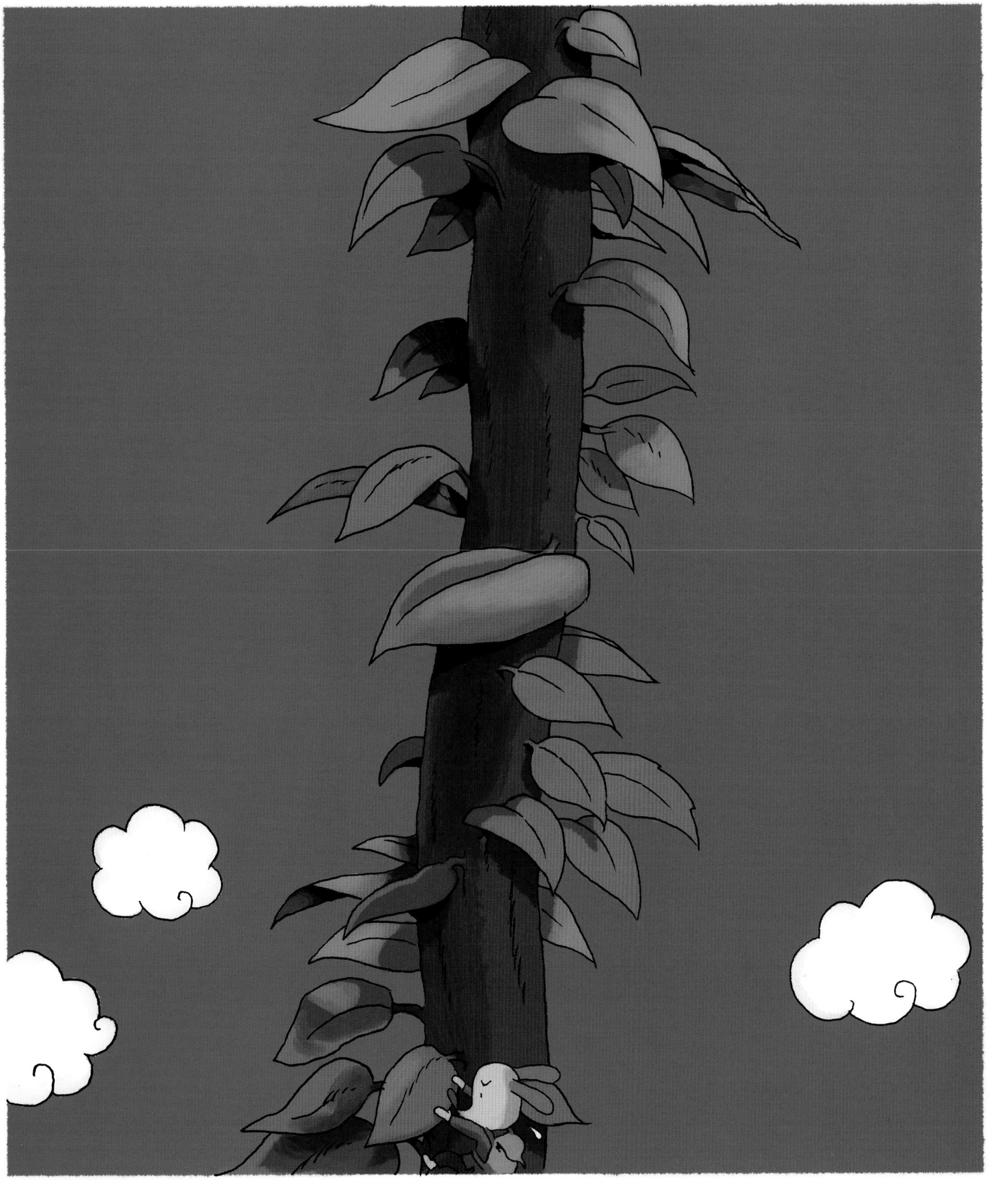

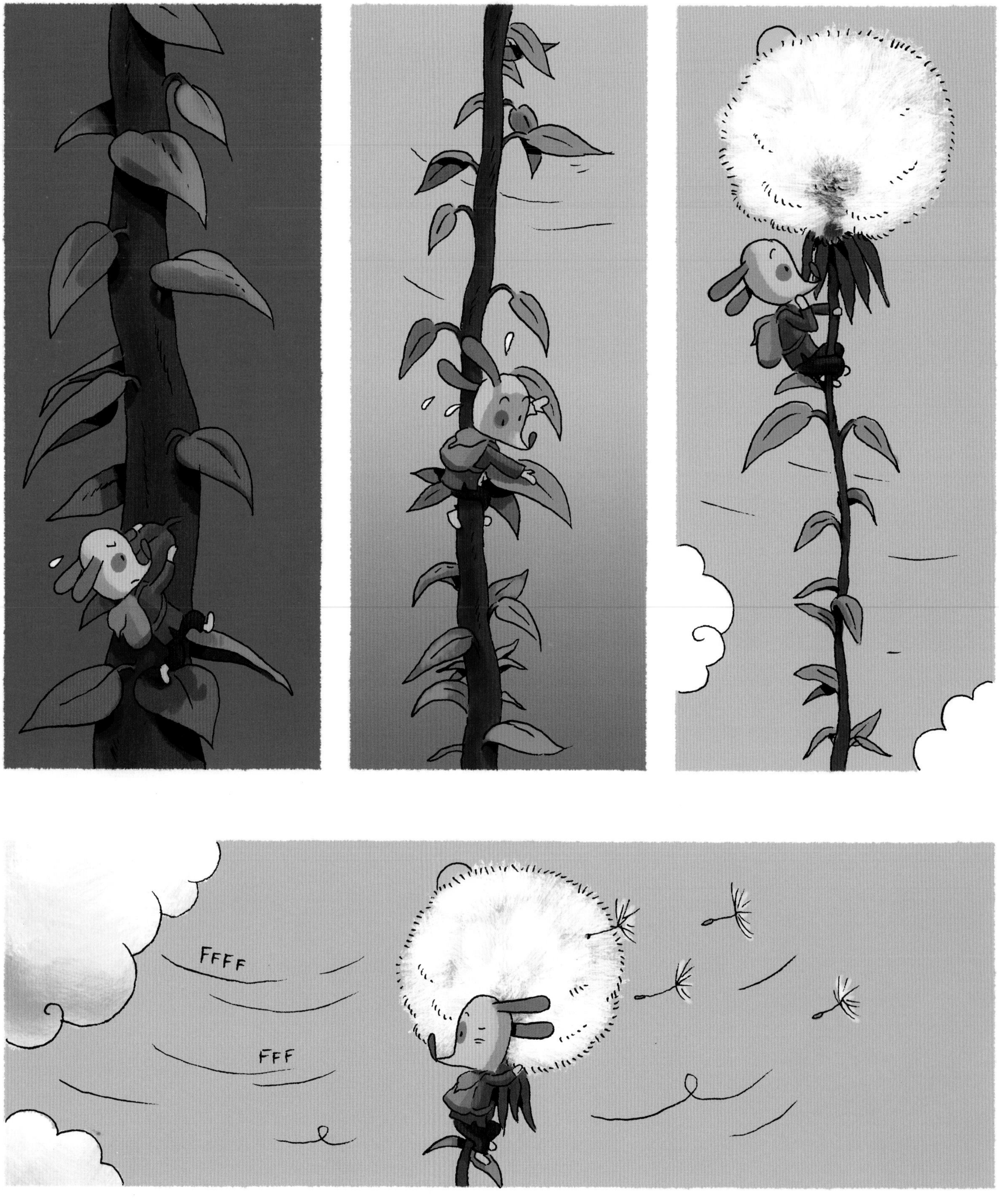
FFFF
FFF

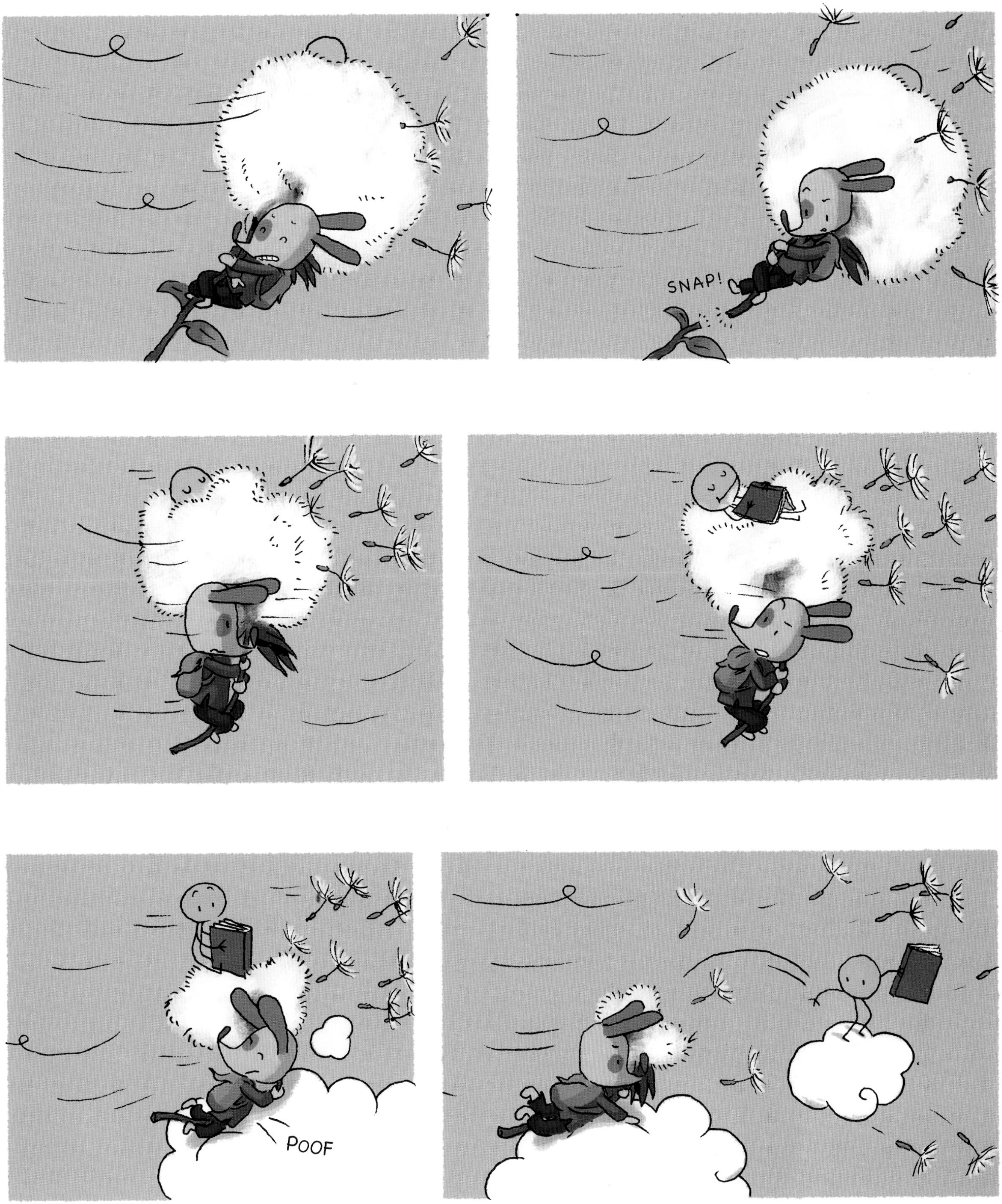
SNAP!
POOF

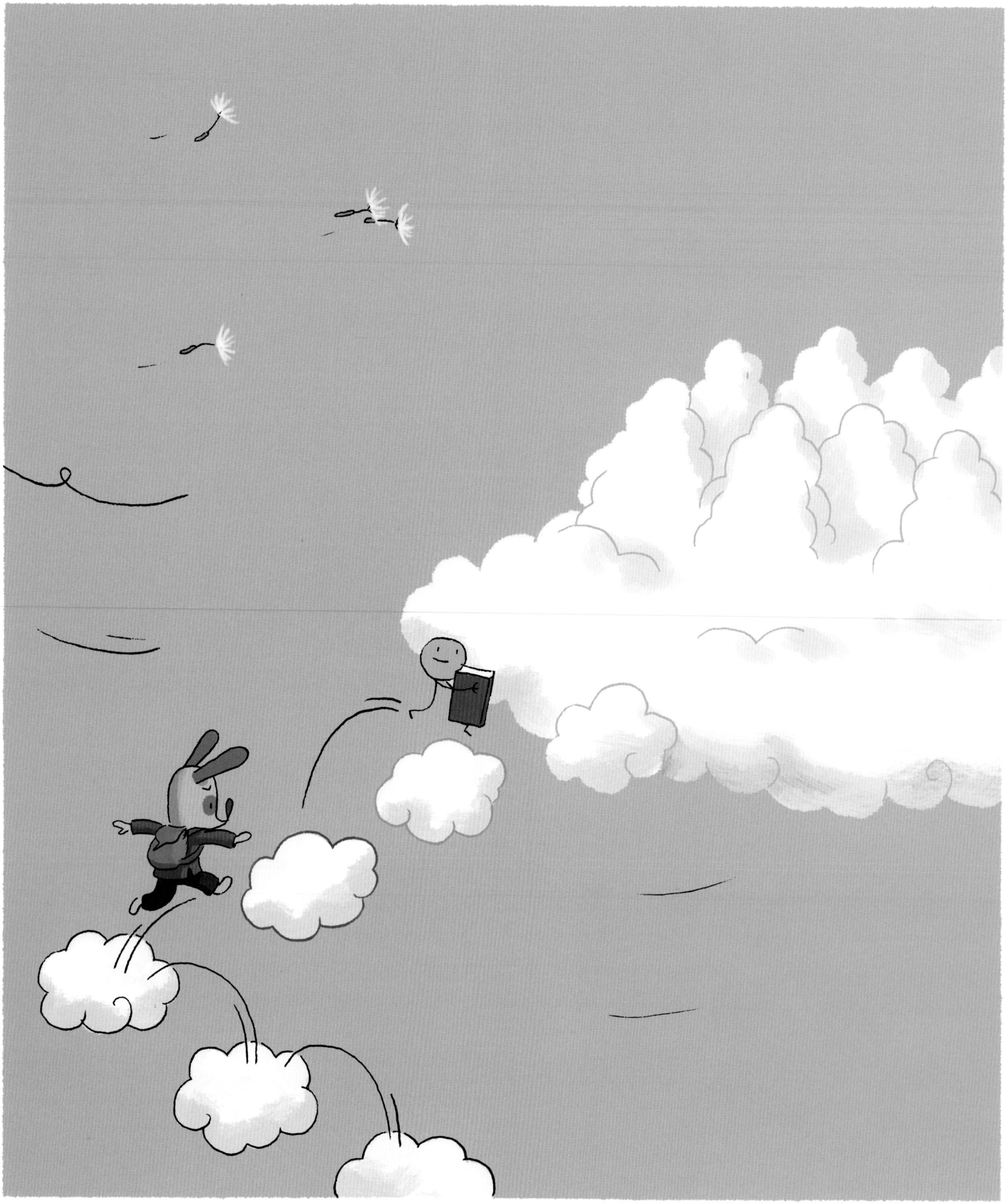

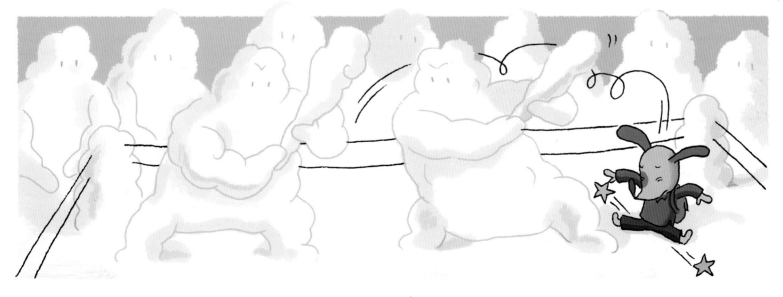

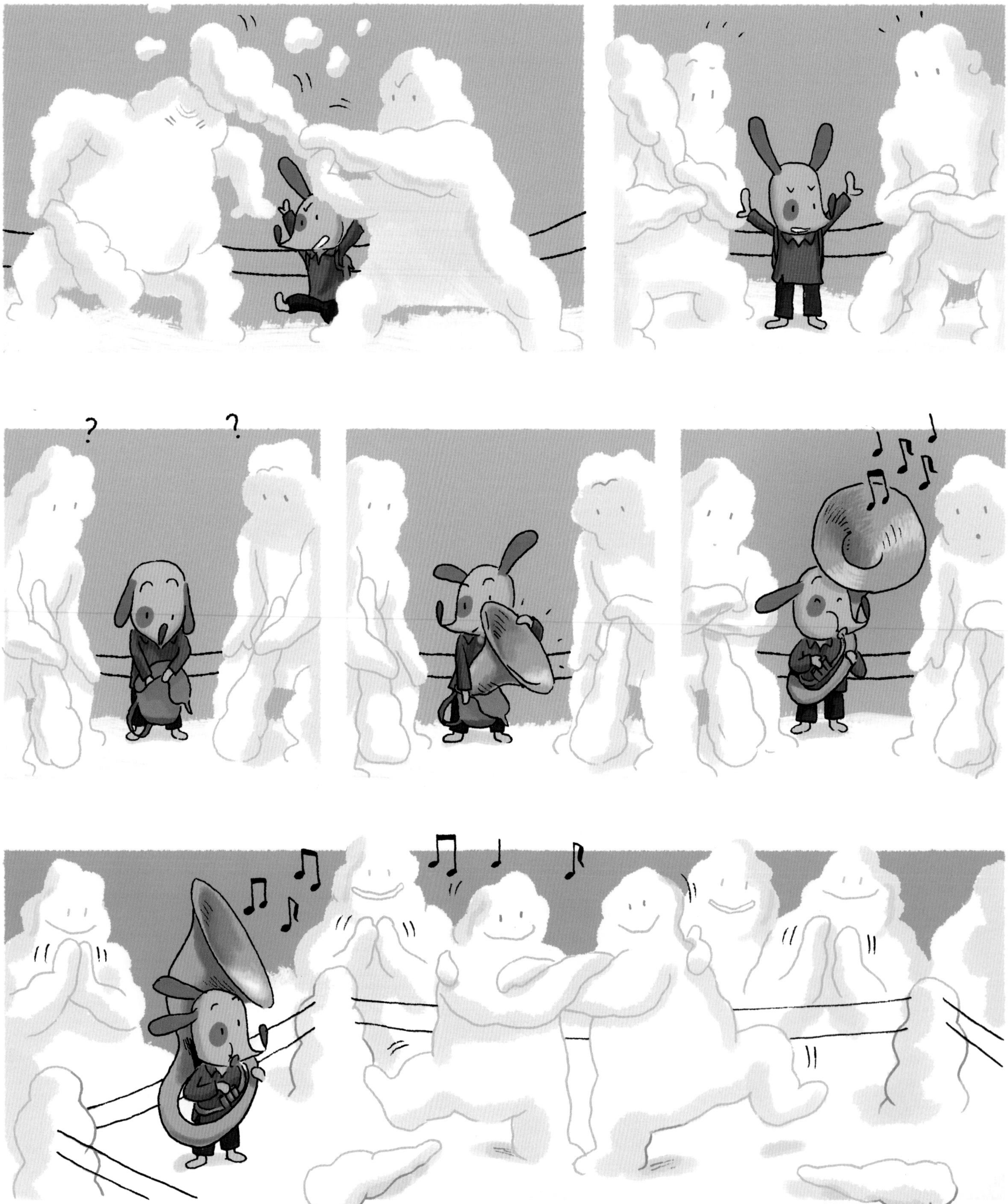
?
?

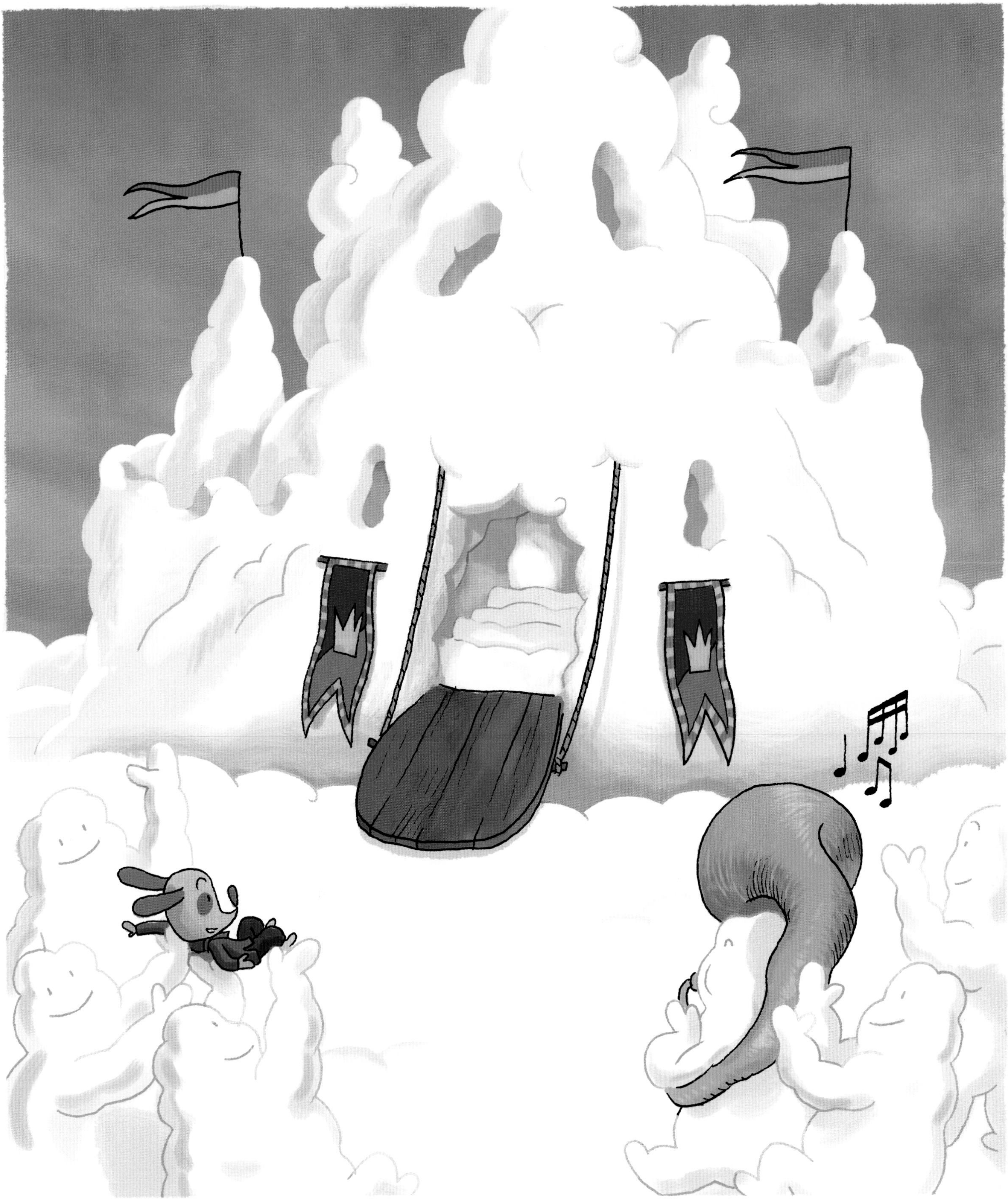

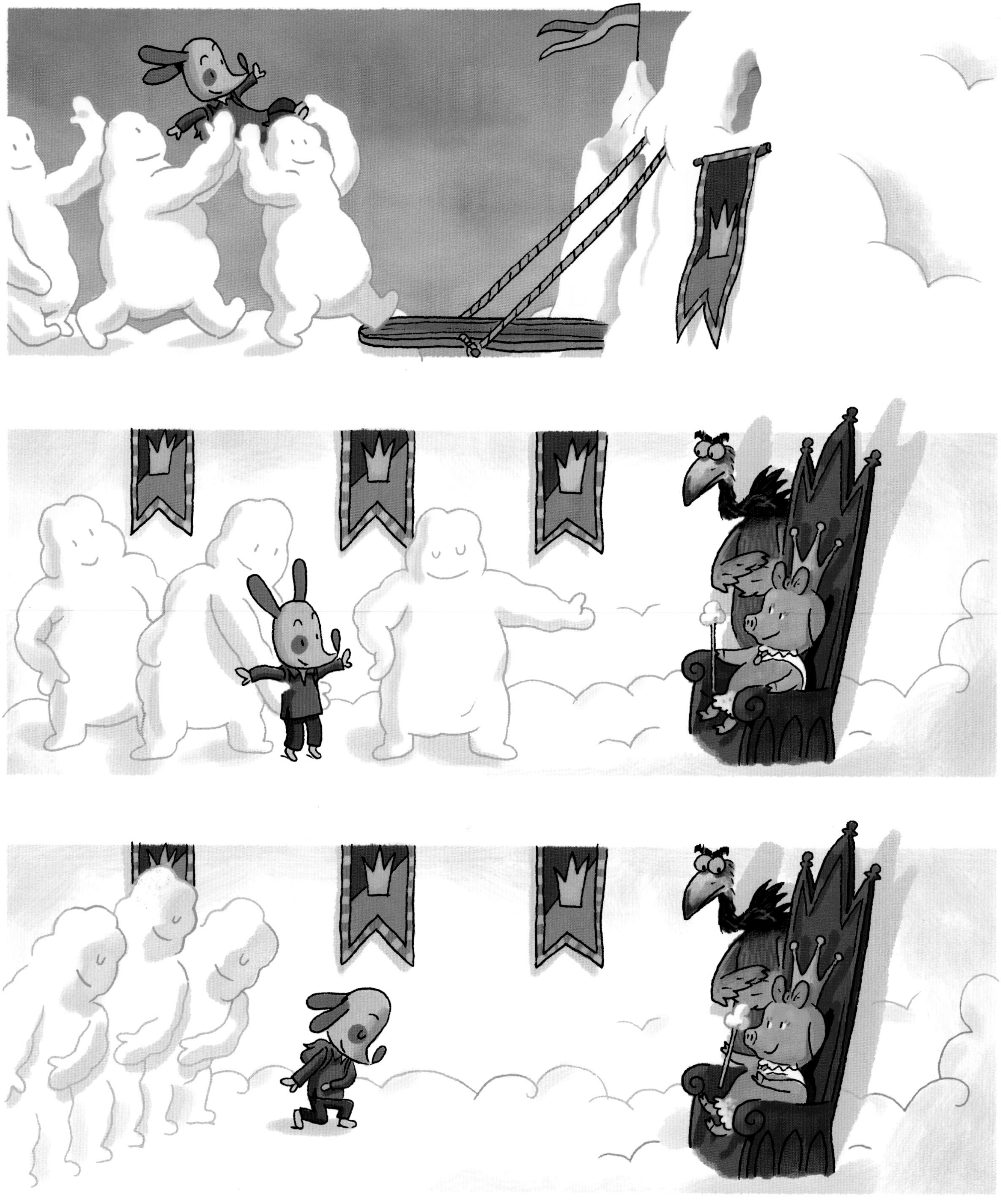

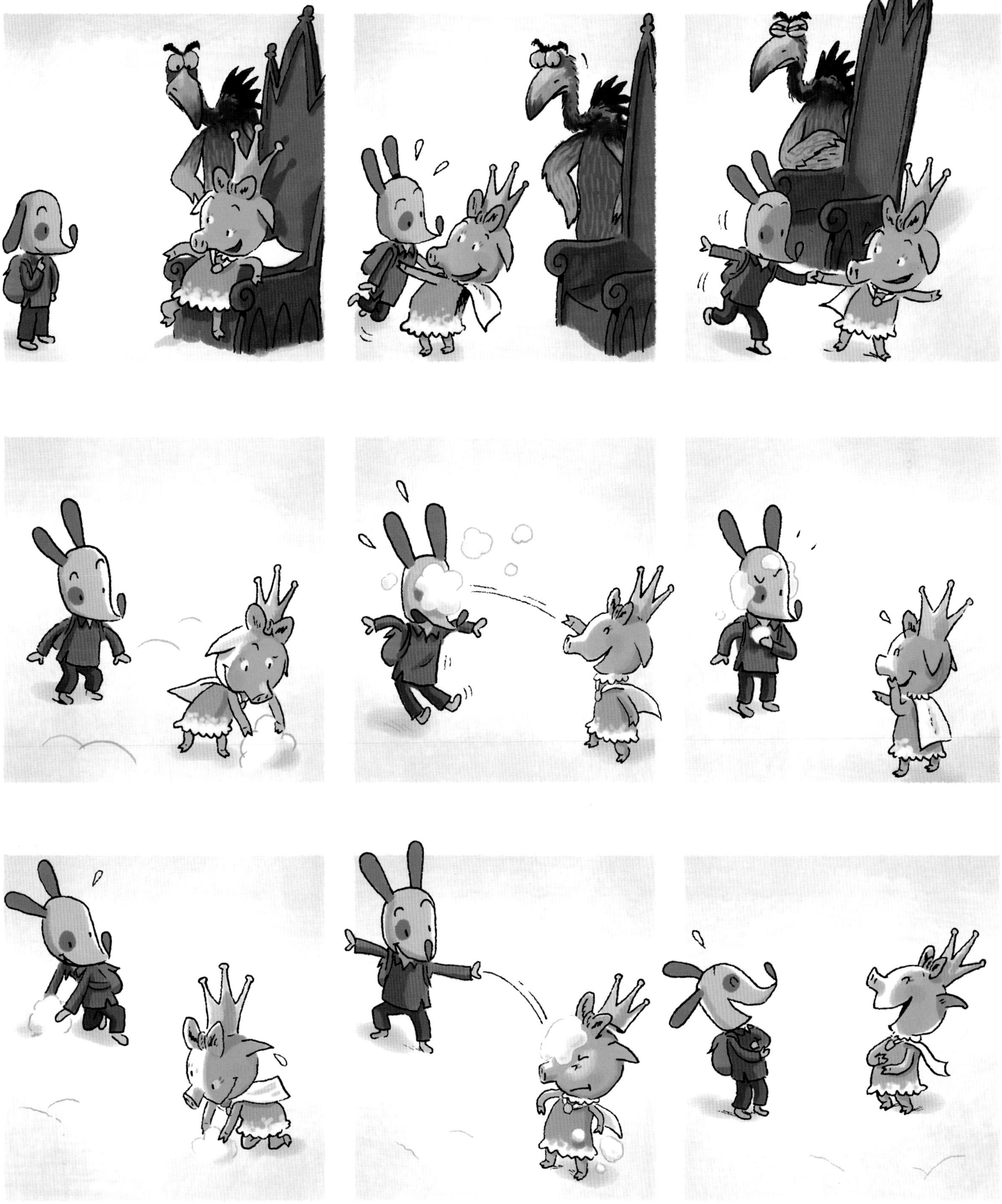

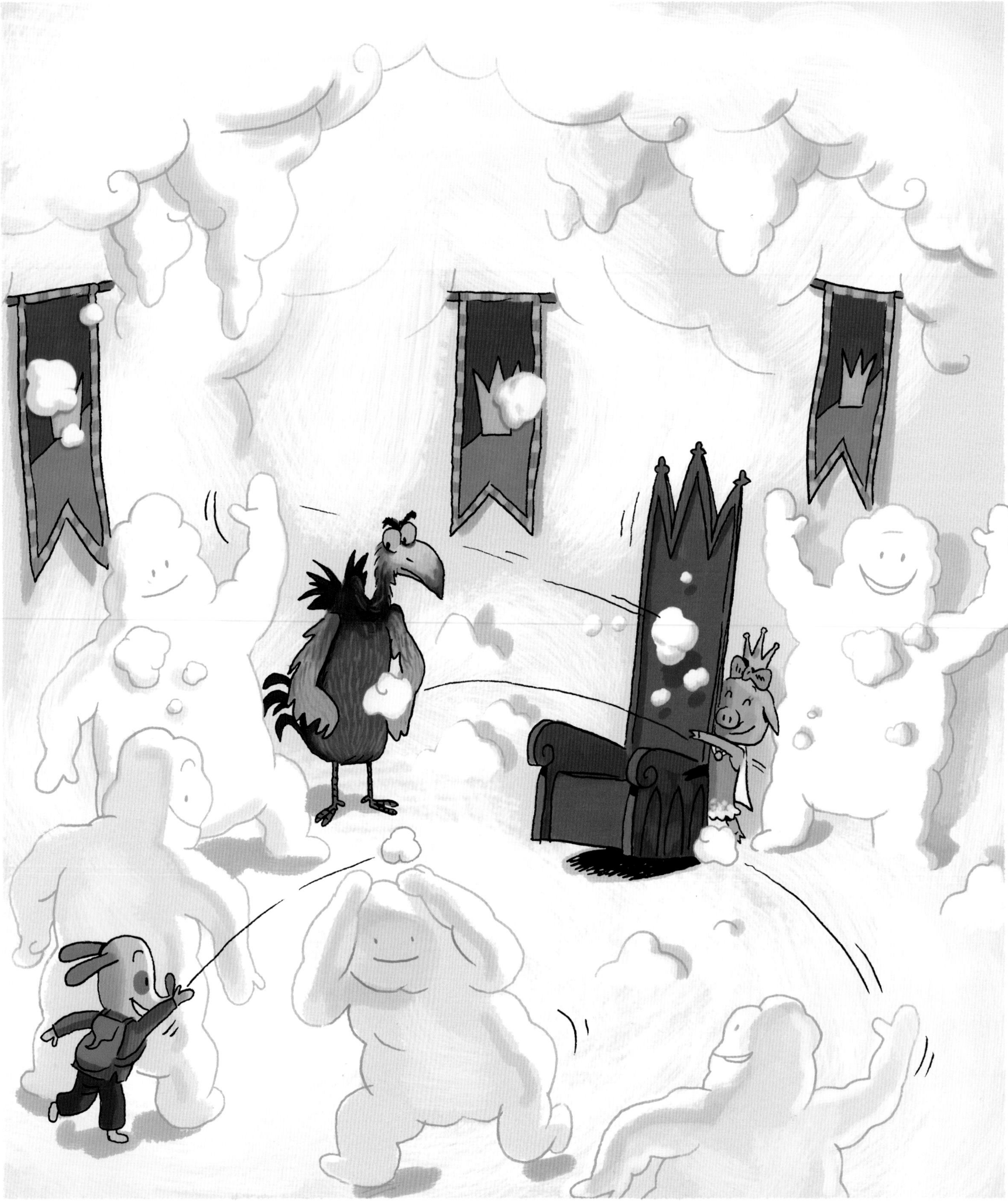

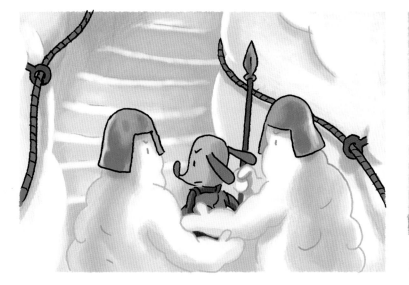

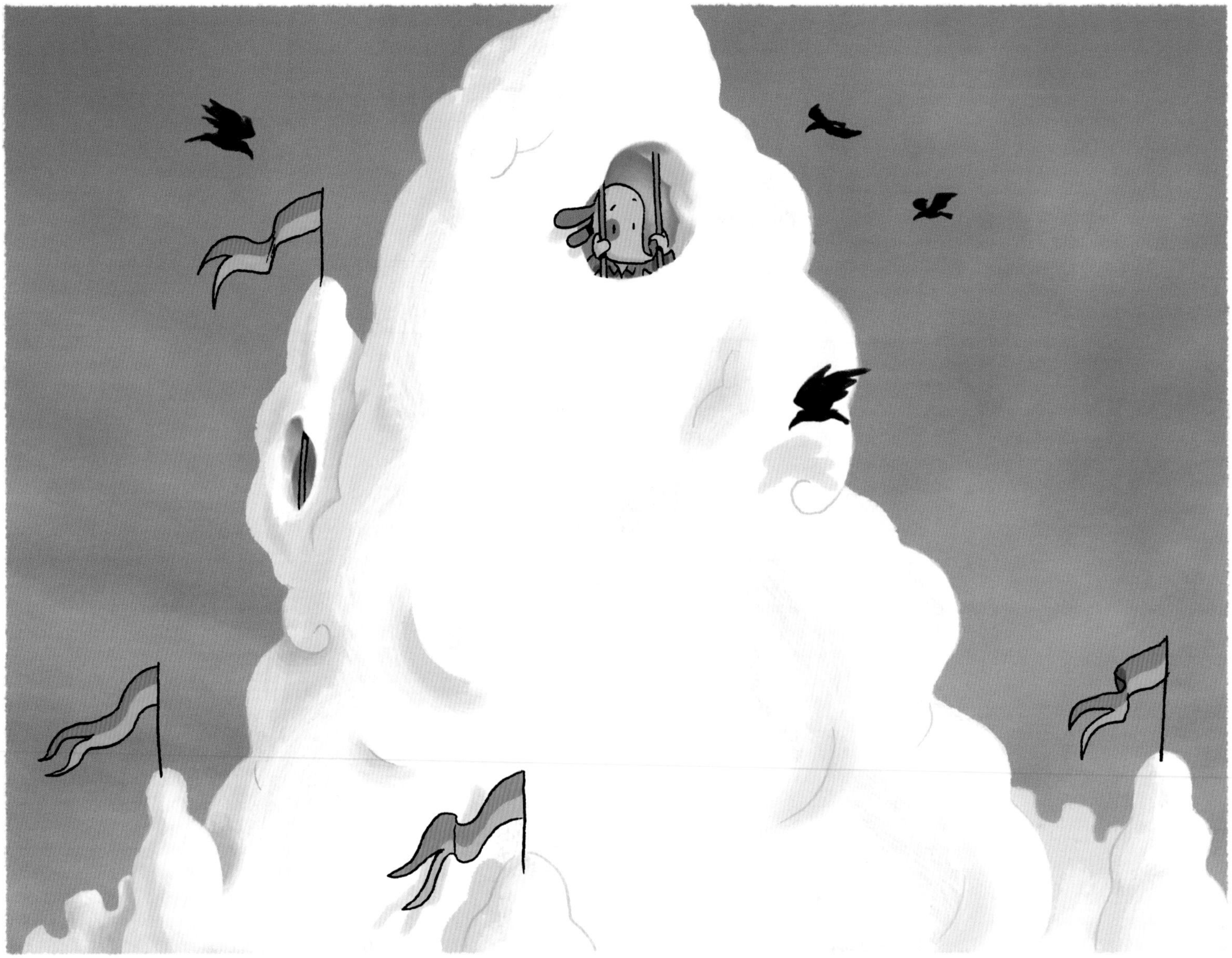

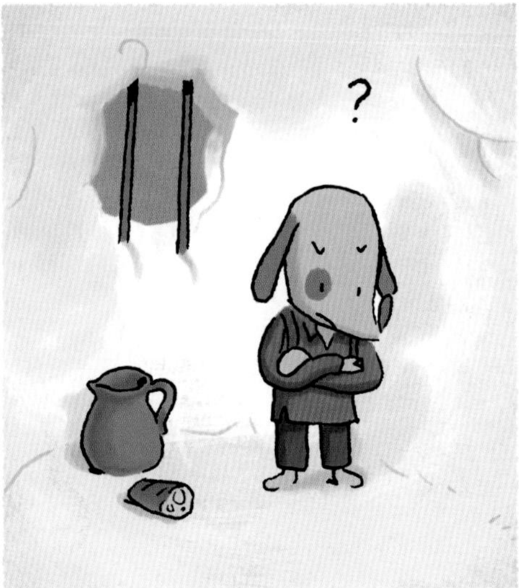
?

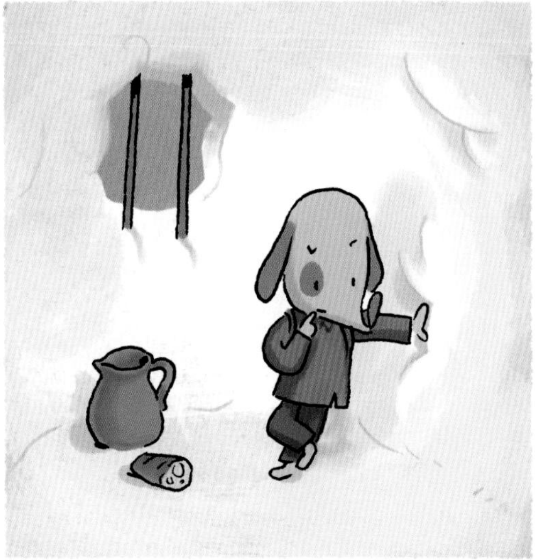

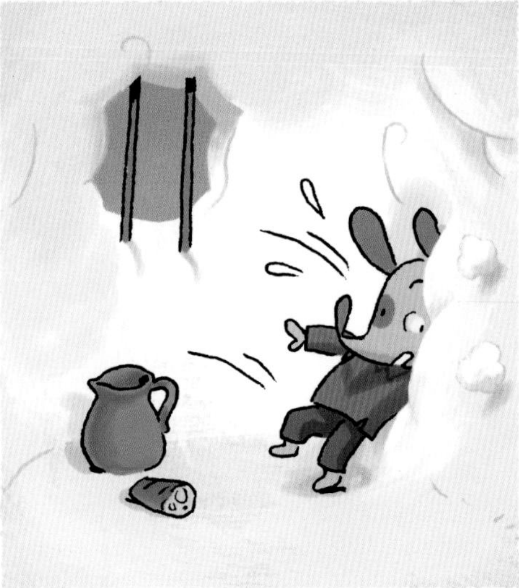

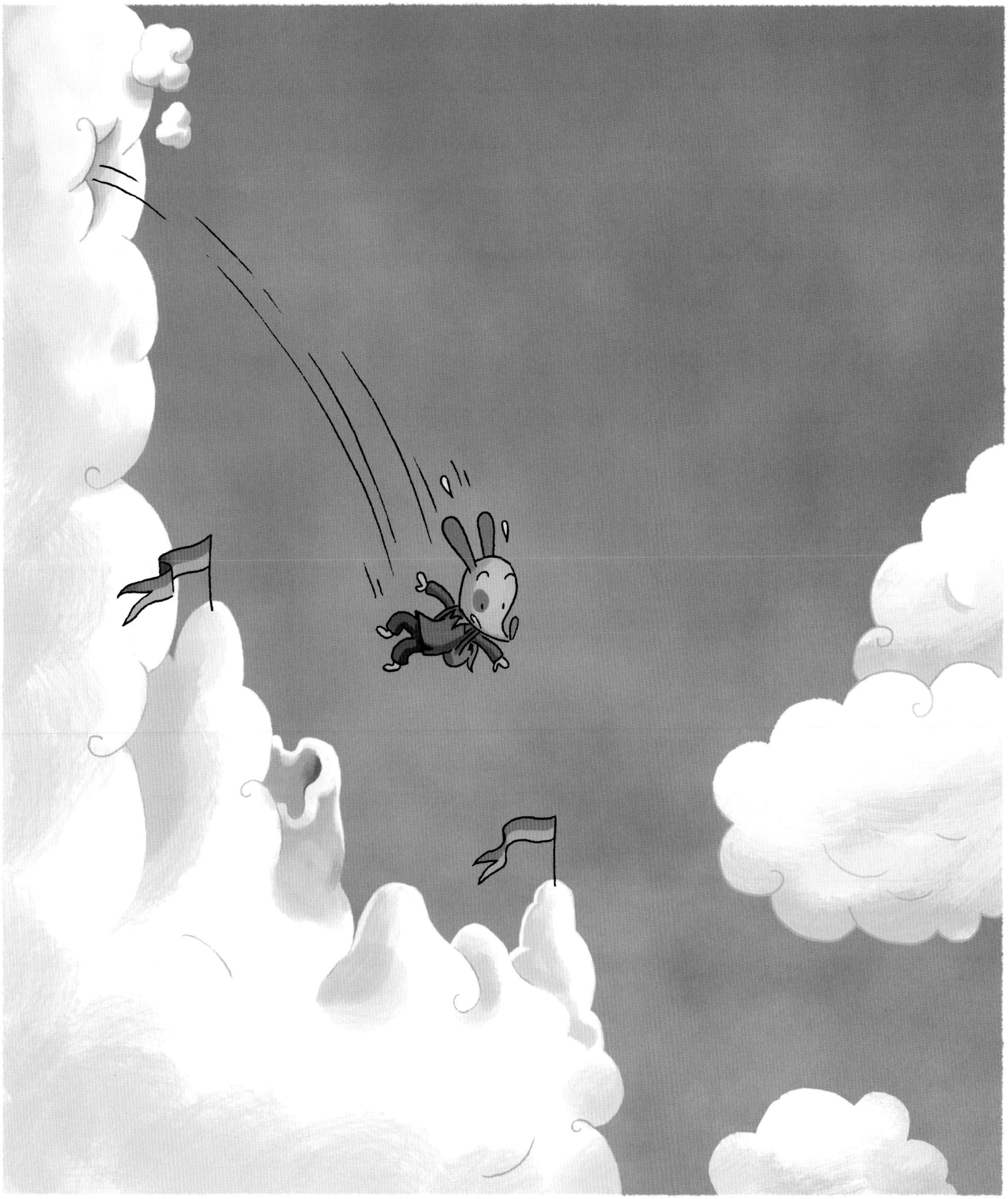

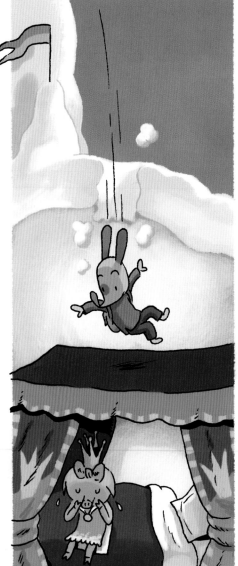

PSSST

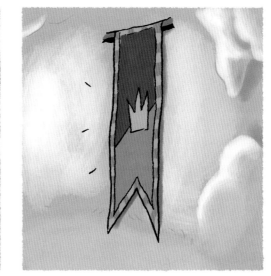

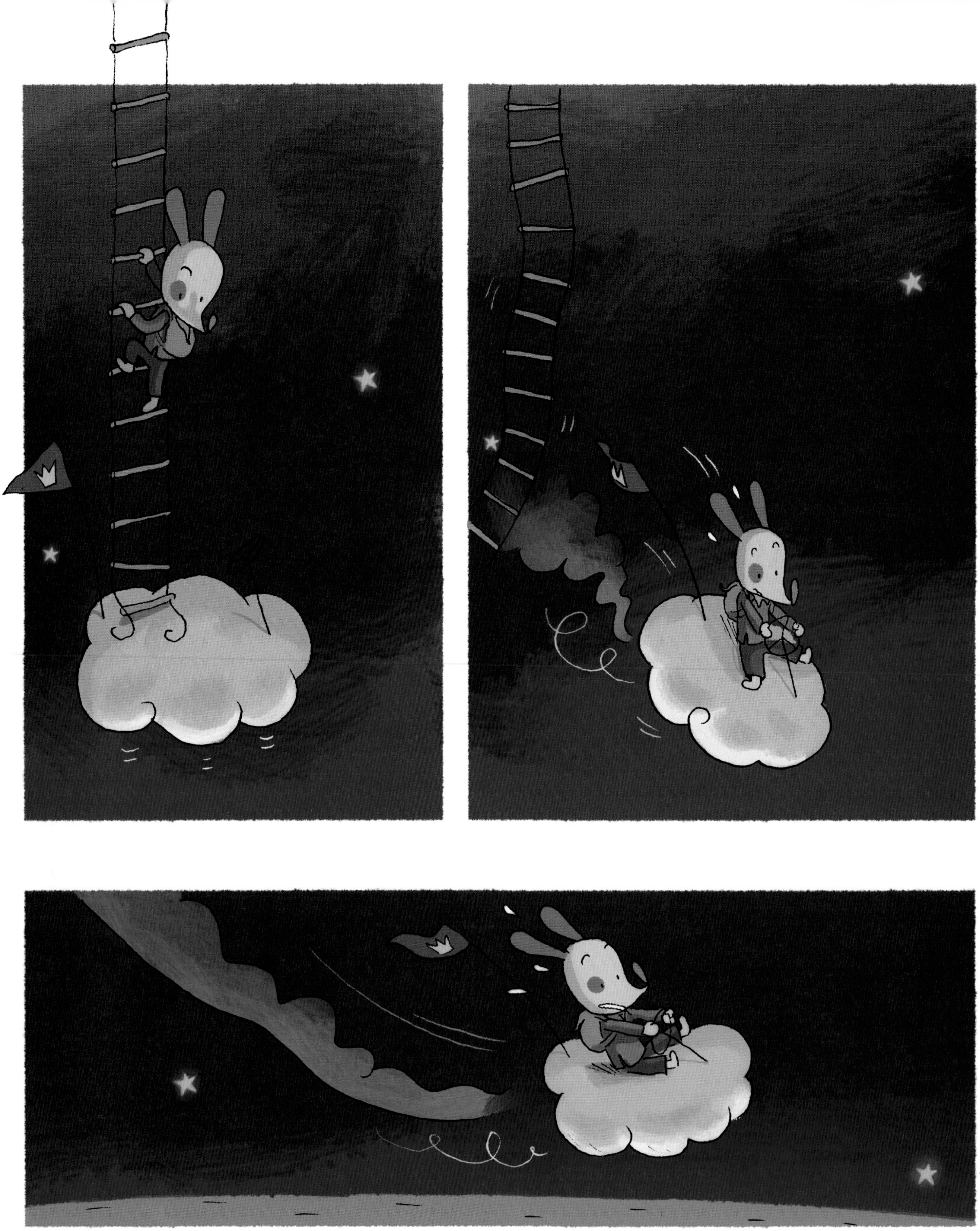

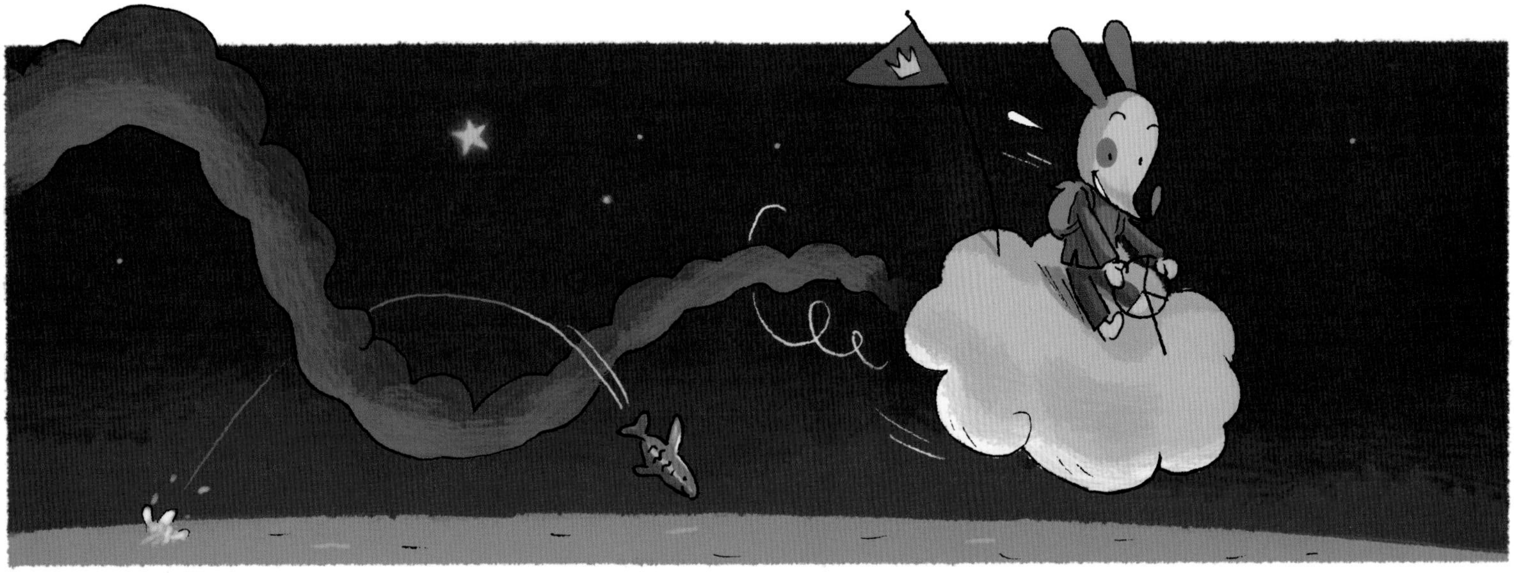

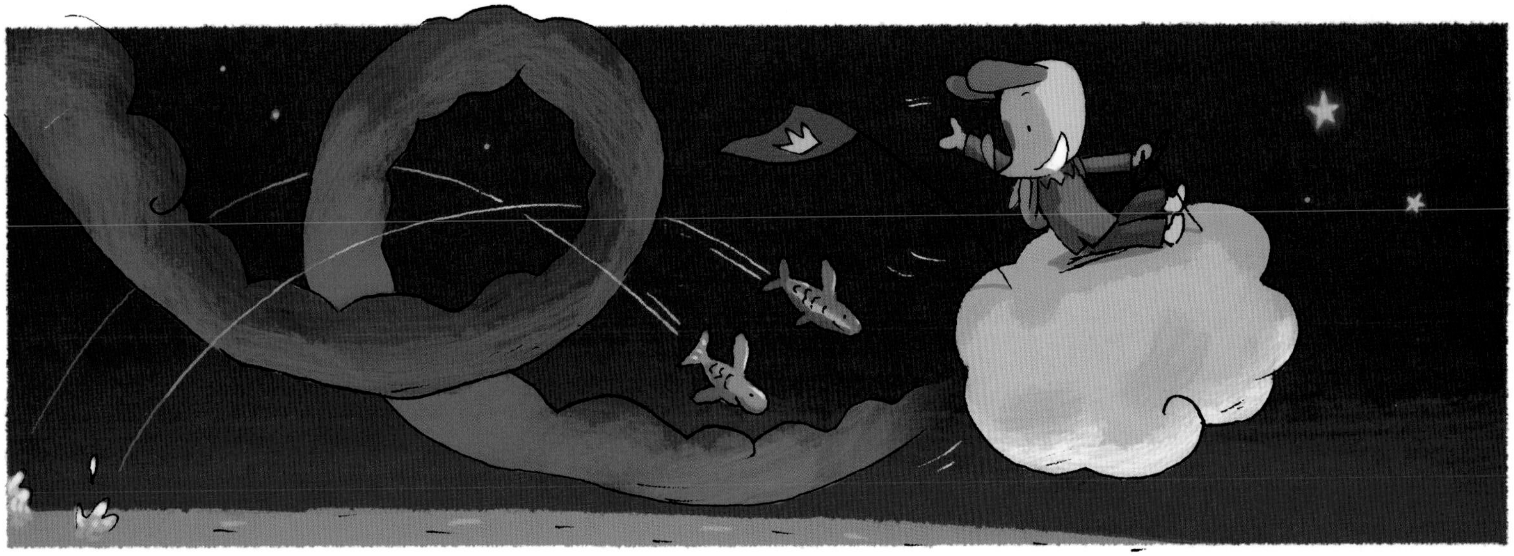

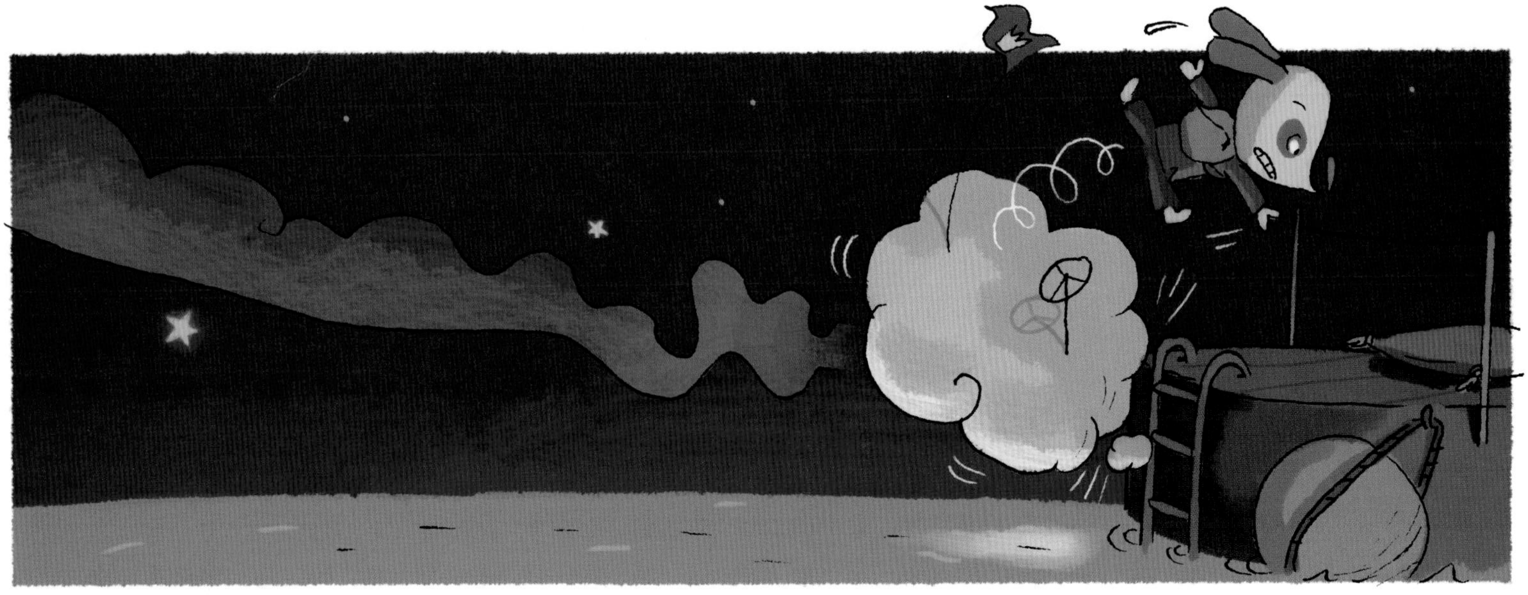

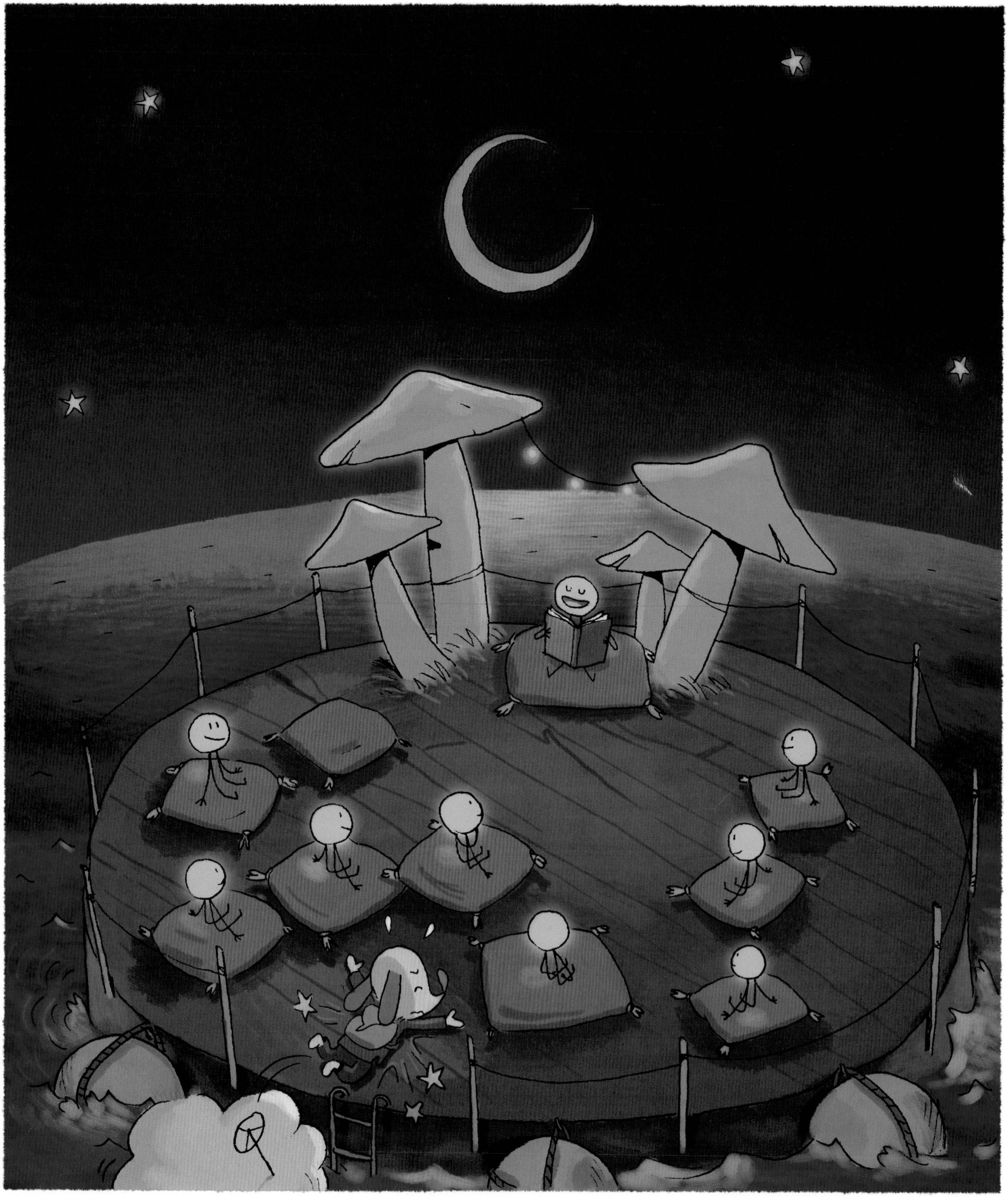

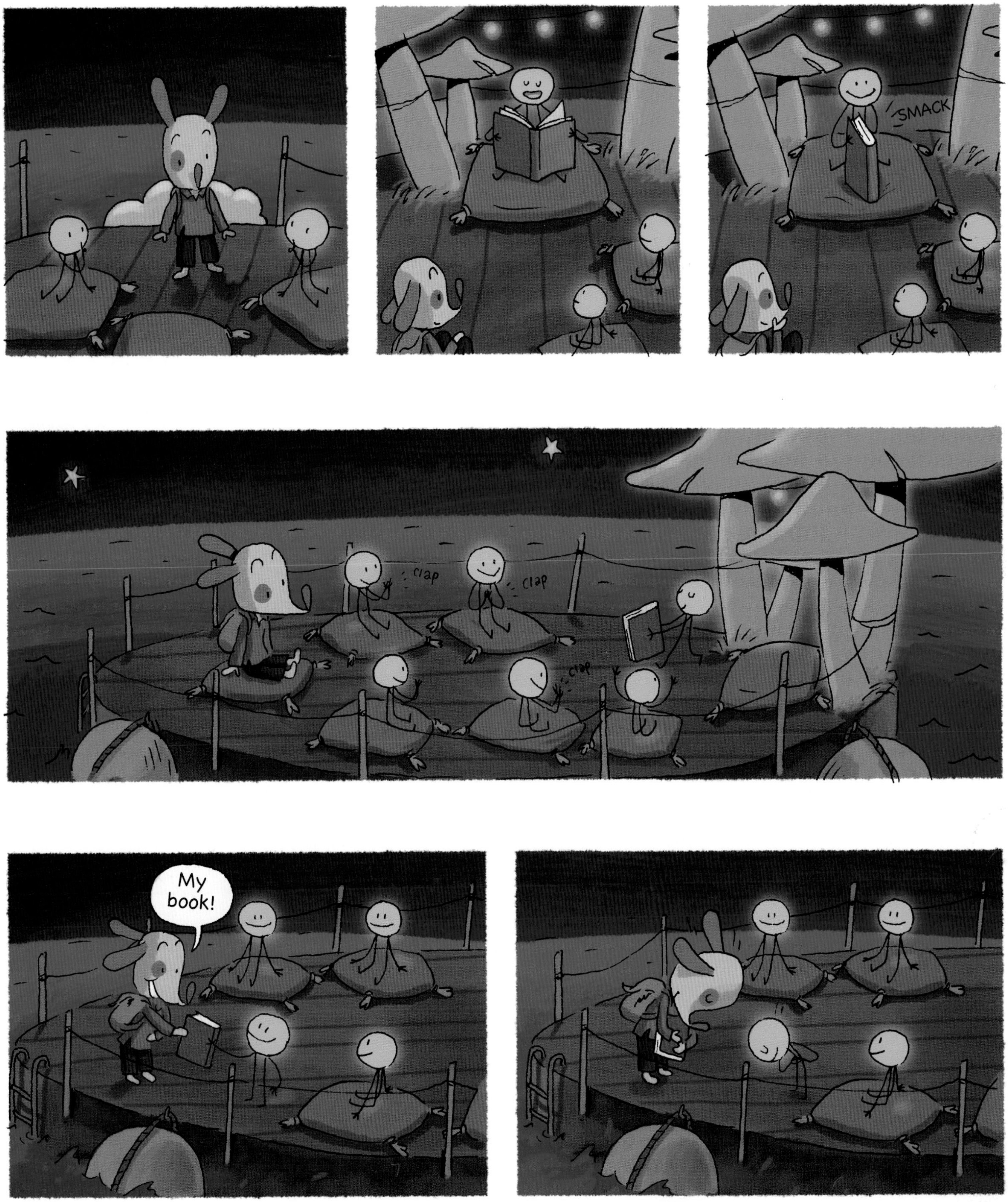
SMACK
clap
clap
clap
My book!

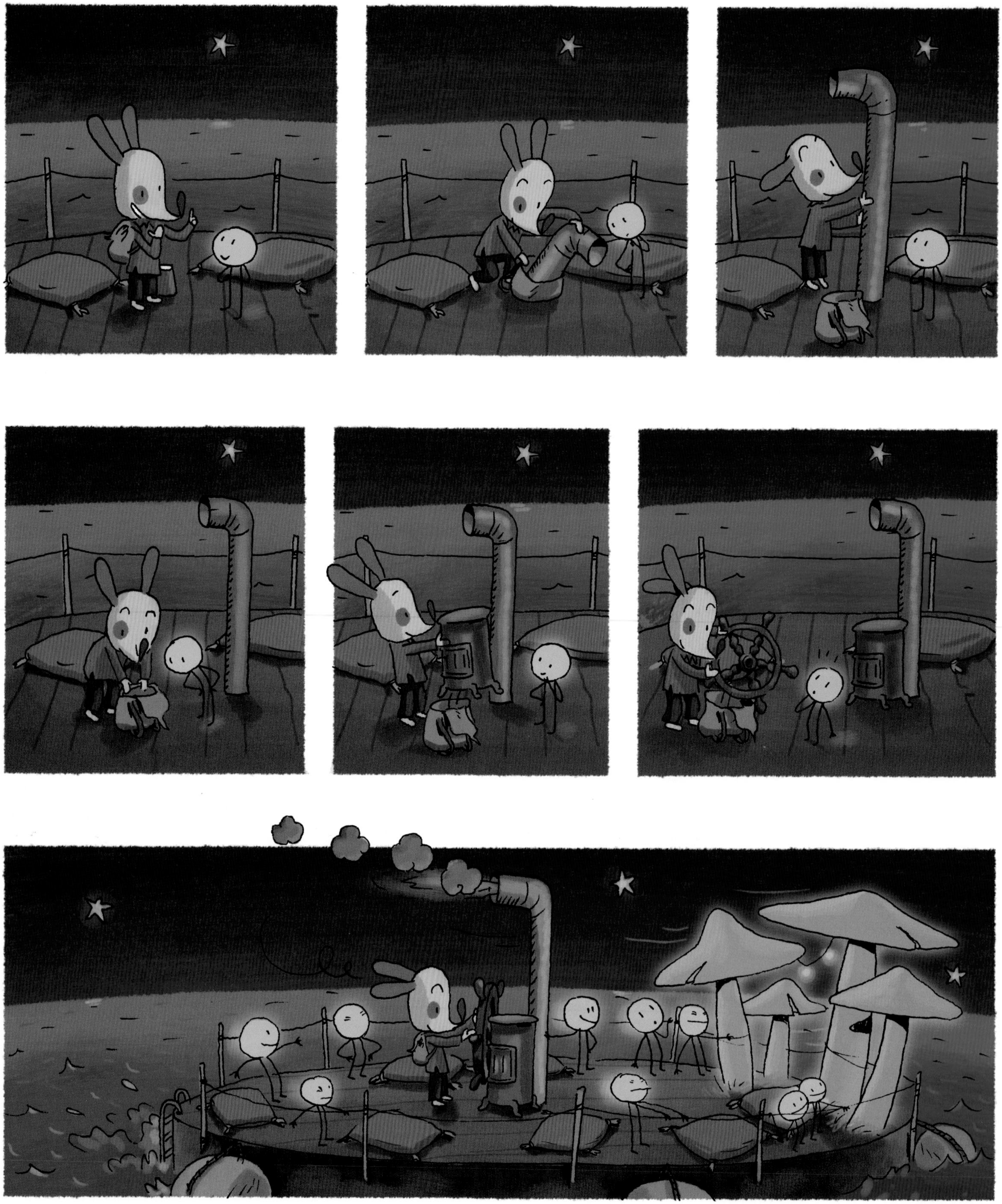

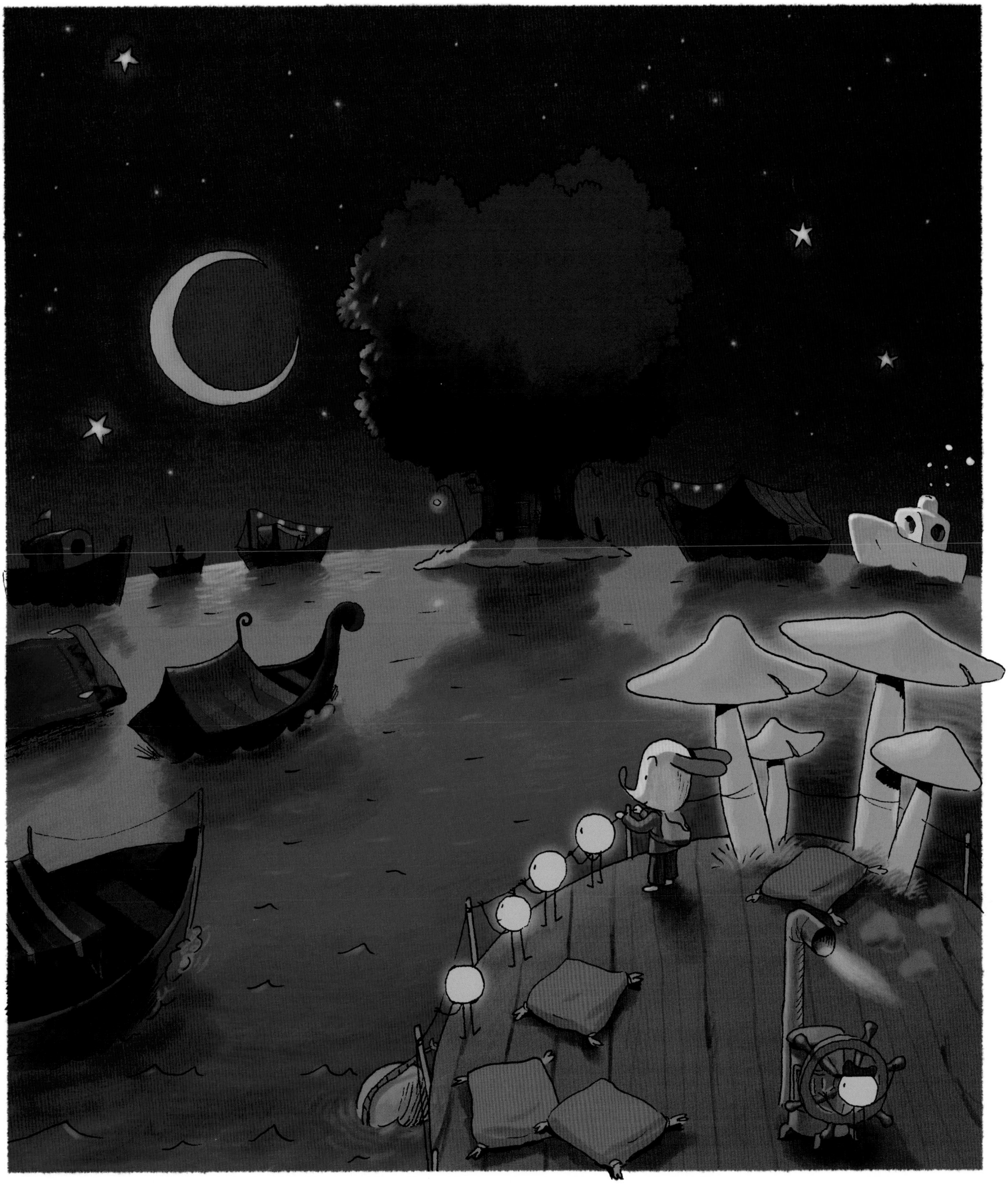

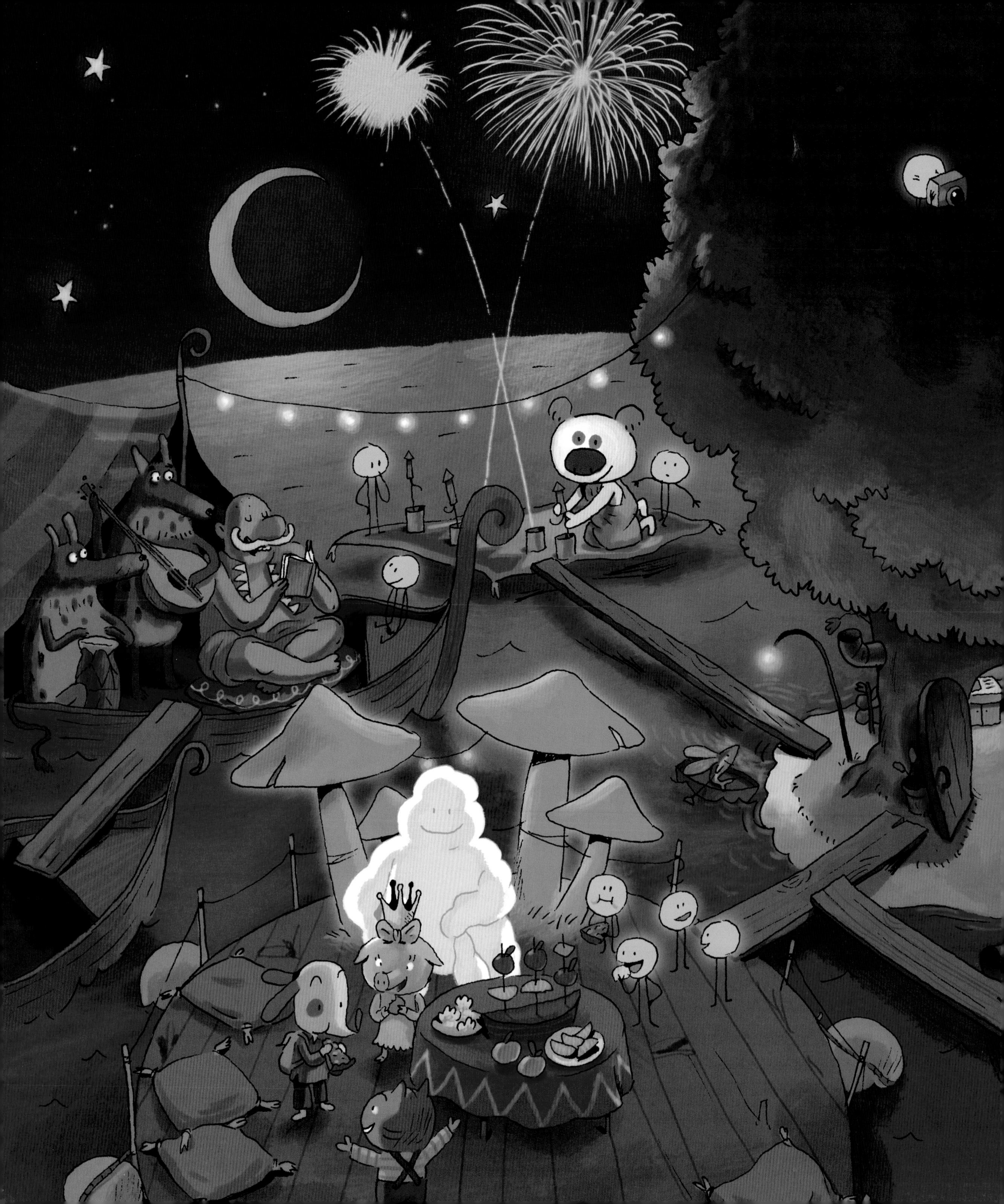

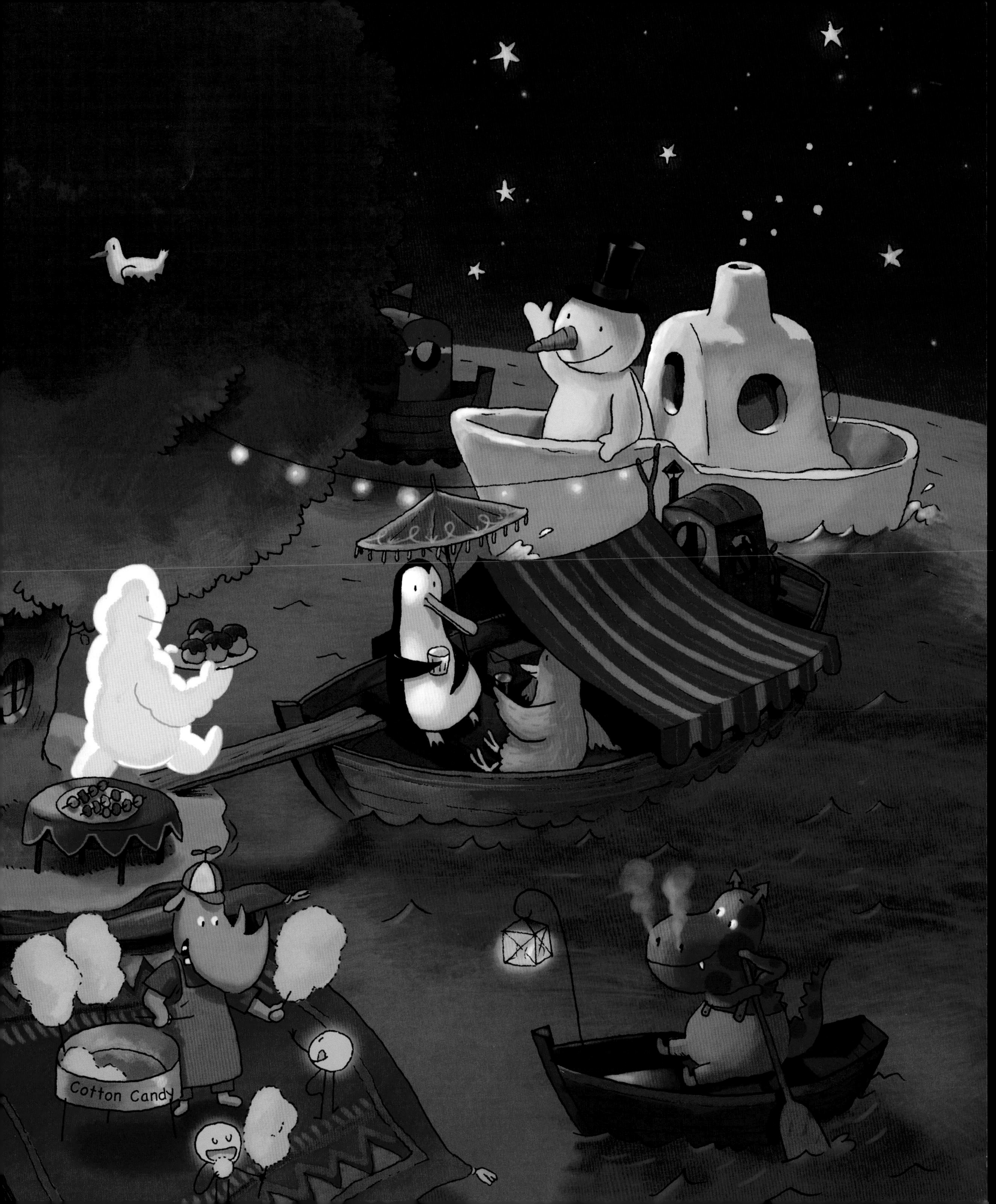
Cotton Candy